INTENTIONAL RISK

MCCULLOUGH MOUNTAIN 8

LYDIA MICHAELS

BAILEY BROWN PUBLISHING

Lydia Michaels

Romance
INTENTIONAL RISK {McCullough Mountain 8 Prequel}
Copyright © 2019 Lydia Michaels

All characters and events in this book are fictitious. Any resemblance to actual persons living or dead is strictly coincidental.
www.LydiaMichaelsBook.com

First E-book Publication: September 2016 as HOW TO LOVE HER
Copyright © 2019 by Lydia Michaels

DEDICATION

To my dad.
Thanks for being there for me when I needed you most.
I love you and all your crazy Italian ways.
You truly are one of my best friends
...and the real Abe Froman.

McCullough Mountain
Publication Order

<u>Almost Priest</u> 1
<u>Beautiful Distraction</u> 2
<u>Irish Rogue</u> 3
<u>British Professor</u> 4
<u>Broken Man</u> 5
<u>Controlled Chaos</u> 6
<u>Hard Fix</u> 7
<u>Intentional Risk</u> 8 or 0.5

Find more McCulloughs in Jasper Falls!

<u>Wake My Heart</u> 1
<u>The Best Man</u> 2
<u>Love Me Nots</u> 3
<u>Pining For You</u> 4
<u>My Funny Valentine</u> 5
<u>Side Squeeze</u> 6
And more…

CHAPTER 1

"Shit. Shit, shit, shit, shit—*shit!*" Sweat beaded on Kate's brow as she huddled over the sink staring down at the tiny stick of doom.

The knob jiggled and her attention jerked to the door, heart palpitating, as she feared someone might burst in—not an unlikely occurrence in this house.

"I'm in here!" she snapped, her frantic eyes jerking back to the pale blue lines growing darker every second.

"What the heck, Kate? You've been in there almost an hour. I have to go."

"Damn it, Kelly, use Braydon's bathroom."

With a huff, her youngest brother stomped down the hall, leaving her alone with nothing but a sinking sensation in the pit of her belly—a sinking sensation and, well, a baby.

"Shit."

Plopping her bottom on the seat of the toilet she stared

at the stick, dismay creeping over her in a cool heat that left her nauseous. Or perhaps that was morning sickness.

"Katie?"

Her eyes widened at the sound of her mother's voice. Frantic to destroy the evidence, she grabbed the pregnancy test—unconcerned with the fact that it had been dunked in urine—and shoved it into her bra. Flushing the toilet, she inspected the small bathroom and turned on the faucet.

Her mother—never easily avoided—knocked on the wooden door again. "Katherine? Are you ill? Kelly said you've been in there a while."

Ah, the pleasures of growing up in a house with nine people. "I'm fine, Mum. I'll be out in a minute." Shutting her eyes, she dowsed her hands with cool water, willing her heart rate to slow.

"Are you constipated, dear?"

"Jesus," she cursed under her breath. "No, Mum. I'm fine."

"Is it your menses?"

"For fuck's sake," she grumbled, shutting off the water. Pasting on a smile, she opened the door. "See. I'm fine."

Her mother frowned. "Well, you look like shite." Pressing the back of her knuckles to Kate's head, her mother scowled. "And clammy, too. Let me take your temperature." Without invitation, her mother grabbed her ears and yanked her forehead to her lips. "You don't feel as though you have a fever." She released her hold of Kate's head and studied her with a concerned scowl.

Anxious to get the pregnancy test out of her bra, Kate pushed into the hall. "I'm not sick. I was just… going to the bathroom. It's impossible to find any privacy in this house."

Her mother chuckled and followed her to her bedroom. "Don't I know it? Seven children don't make it easy. With so many there's no time to make more, being that your father and I need to trek into the woods for a moment alone."

"Mum, no one wants to hear that."

"Well, the wildlife hasn't a choice. Children bursting like bees out of a hive in this house. I'm lucky I don't catch a tick bite." A flutter of footsteps sounded in the hall and her head cocked to the side like an alert beagle. Suddenly, she turned and shouted, "Kelly! Don't you leave this house without cleaning that room, you hear?" Her attention returned to Kate. "That boy is a slug, leaves a trail wherever he goes. Found a cup in his room yesterday that could have won a ribbon at the science fair. Why the Lord thought to punish me with five boys I haven't a clue."

Ignoring her mother, Kate sorted through her drawers searching for a decent shirt. If she was going to see Nick she couldn't go to him looking like some reject from *Little House on the Prairie.*

Frustrated at her limited selection of clothing, she growled. "I need new clothes." She slammed the drawer and went to the closet.

Her mother busied herself collecting laundry off the floor. "They're having a sale at McGinty's this week."

Kate rolled her eyes. "I don't want to buy my clothes where Daddy gets his coveralls and guns, Mum. I need something stylish."

"Oh," her mother hummed. "Is this about that boy you've been seeing? He's quite a looker. I bet he draws some fierce competition from the other girls."

"Mum!" Like she needed a reminder of how popular Nick was.

Her mother shrugged, holding an armful of towels and jeans. "Well, he's handsome. I can't be the only one who sees it. You don't go to a school for the blind, love. He probably gets his fair share of attention."

"Thanks. Like I wasn't insecure enough." The sad part was she was right. Everyone saw Nick and he noticed. He noticed *a lot*.

"Oh, don't be so down on yourself, dearie. A real man likes a woman with a little room in her trunk."

Kate stilled and slowly pivoted. Her mother wasn't paying attention to her reaction or even remotely aware of how offensive she could be sometimes. "You have no filter."

Holding Kate's clothing over her fuller frame as she admired herself in the mirror, her mother was too invested in her own fantasy world to see her daughter was in a crisis. Kate looked over her shoulder and analyzed her butt, wondering if it was above average. Not like it mattered anyway. Her body was going to swell up like a puffer fish over the next few months.

"I see nothing wrong with the clothes you've got," her

mother muttered, admiring a green blouse that was almost five years old. "This is nice."

"Mum, that's from eighth grade. I'm graduating."

"If we were the same size I'd be begging to borrow these things."

Two months. In two months she be finished high school and able to move out on her own. However, without a job that would be difficult and her new predicament didn't make things any easier.

Oh, God. What am I going to do?

She needed to go to the pharmacy outside of town and buy another test. That's what she needed to do. Snatching the blouse from her mother she asked, "Did you talk to Daddy about the secretary position at the lumberyard?"

"It slipped my mind. He should be home any minute though. Why don't you ask him? You know he can't say no to you."

That might change once he realized she'd broken the big cardinal rule of Irish Catholic daughters. She couldn't face him right now. "I'm meeting Cheryl at the movies in twenty minutes," she lied. "Can I have some money?"

Her mother scoffed. "What do I look like, a bank?" Her attention jerked toward the hall. "Colin! Where are you off to?"

Her brother poked his head through the doorway. "I promised Father Mark I'd run a load of firewood over to the monastery for next season."

"Okay then. Light a candle for your brother." It needed

no clarification the brother she referred to was Kelly. She was always lighting candles for him.

Kate took the opportunity to slip past her mother and escape further inquisition. Her younger siblings were crowded around the kitchen table pretending to do homework. Luke flicked a paper football at Finn as Sheilagh, the youngest, squirmed in her seat. Braydon was the only one actually writing in his books.

"Where you going, Kate?" Sheilagh called, twiddling her pencil as she studied her big sister like a hawk.

"Nowhere. Mind your own business."

Unfortunately, her little sister's question drew the attention of Luke, Finn, and Braydon. Ignoring them, she helped herself to her mother's pocketbook hanging by the door. Luke, seeing her take the twenty-dollar bill, nearly blew her cover.

"Oooh, I'm telling Mum."

Kate sent him a scathing glance as she stuffed the wallet back in the bag. "She knows. Do your homework." Folding the bill in half, she slid it into her pocket just before the screen door opened. Her stomach bottomed out as her father stepped into the kitchen, parking his plaid lunch pail on the counter where he always left it.

Sheilagh bounded out of her seat and leapt into his arms and Kate took the opportunity to slip out the back before the screen door had a chance to shut. When she was behind the wheel of her Beretta, she let out a relieved breath.

"Katie Girl," her father called and she quickly turned

the key in the ignition, but it was too late. He met her at the car door. "Where are you running off to? We're about to have dinner."

"I'm meeting Cheryl—"

"Not tonight. You've missed dinner almost every night this week. Come back inside and have dinner with your family."

"But—"

He arched a brow and she sagged in the seat, shutting off the car. Her parents didn't understand how crucial it was to get to town. Cheryl wasn't even part of the equation. She was just the alibi and a very real complication that had once been her friend.

If Kate didn't make it to town eventually, Cheryl would. And while she never used to be in competition with her once best friend, things had changed drastically since Cheryl had gone on a date with Nick. *Kate's Nick.* But he wasn't hers any more than he was Cheryl's or Connie's or Madeline's or Jill's.

Following her father back into the house, she struggled through a noisy, drawn out family dinner and knew she'd get no sleep knowing her once friend was likely sealing the deal with her sort of boyfriend. Lying in bed that night, Kate stared at the ceiling, worrying about what might happen if the test was accurate. She needed to buy another one to be sure and they weren't cheap.

She couldn't be pregnant. She had plans and none of those plans had anything to do with children just yet. Not to mention, if she got pregnant her father would freak out. Her parents weren't the sanest people in Center County. Far from it. But as much as outsiders assumed her mother was the crazy one, her father would go ape shit if he found out she was having sex.

Images of Nick being bullied down a wedding aisle with her father's shotgun jabbed in his back didn't seem too far-fetched.

"Oh, God," she mumbled into the dark. If she could just take another test, prove it was a false positive, she'd never have sex again. Ever.

CHAPTER 2

Kate stared down at the six pregnancy tests in horror. *Six!* She'd taken one to the bathroom during every class and now she had six positives to show. As a stall door slammed and she stood alone in the locker room bathroom, she let her last shred of hope go and dropped her face into her palms. "Fuck me."

This wasn't how it was supposed to happen. She was supposed to have a year on her own. She wanted her own apartment, a real job, and freedom. She was supposed to be independent and have several mad love affairs before getting tied down. This changed everything. Not to mention the way her parents would look at her. Oh, they were going to be so disappointed.

New voices echoed in the locker room and she swept the tests up and tossed them into the trash like a handful of lost dreams. Disoriented, she grabbed her bag and kept her head down as she sidled past the cheerleaders getting ready for practice. Lost in her thoughts and not paying attention to her surroundings, she pushed through the gymnasium door and slammed into a hard, *sweaty* body.

Her purse fell out of her grip as pain exploded in her face. It took everything she had not to burst into tears, that sharp crash sending her dangerously close to the edge.

"Are you okay?"

Shaken, she merely registered his height and girth, her main focus on the radiating pain.

"I'm so sorry. I didn't see you," the jock continued, his voice muffled under his helmet.

Reaching down to retrieve her purse, her head smacked right into his oversized shoulder pad sending another splash of blinding pain through her head. "Jesus!"

"Oh my gosh!" he blurted, pulling off his mud packed helmet. Dark, startled eyes stared at her, as she shook off what she hoped was the last of his assault. His black hair was damp with sweat, pressed into sloppy disarray and matted to his temples. The scent of earth and soil nearly did her in.

Her fingers brushed her cheekbone where it had collided with his jersey as her other hand held the top of her head. *Anyone else want to hurt me?*

She blinked as the sting transcended into burning tears, but she forced them back. "I'm fine." Her vision blurred, the scent of soggy grass still turning her stomach. Her brow pinched tight, a headache already taking hold.

"Uh…" He took a step forward. "Why don't you sit down for a minute?"

"Okay." Dizzy and jarred from the *two* collisions, she unsteadily nodded. Without considering anything more than the fact she didn't want to pass out, she lowered herself to the gymnasium floor.

"I meant on the bleachers, but this works too." He took a knee and frowned. "You might get a shiner. I'm really sorry." Reaching behind his hip, he retrieved her purse and set it in her lap. "I should get you some ice."

Shaking off the pain, she waved away his concern. "That's really not necessary. I'm fine. I wasn't watching where I was going." She moved to get off the floor and he caught her arm as her equilibrium wavered.

"Wait another minute before standin'. You cracked me pretty hard, champ." He knocked his knuckles on the plated shoulder pad stretching his jersey. "These aren't soft."

When she squinted at him, but made no reply, he said, "I'm Ant."

She frowned at the little syllable of a name. "Ant? Like the bug?"

He laughed. "No, Ant as in Anthony."

Now that her head had stopped spinning, she finally got a good look at him and wondered why she didn't recognize him. "Are you new here?"

"Transferred in last fall. My family moved here from Philadelphia."

That explained his slight accent. When he spoke he seemed to swallow his *L*'s and *T*'s. "You talk fast."

His dark eyes shifted as if considering her comment. "I think I talk at a normal speed."

She laughed. "*Tawk?*"

"Tawk," he repeated and frowned. Then he mumbled, "Tawk. Tawk. *Tallllk*. Now it sounds weird no matter how I say it. You okay to stand up now?"

His accent was the strangest twang she'd ever heard. "Yeah, I think I'm okay to stand up *nail*."

He pursed his lips. "Bit of a ball breaker, aren't ya?"

"Not usually." Maybe it was the two thwacks to the head.

He grinned, his teeth flashing white against his tan skin. "Here, I'll help you stand, smart ass."

Taking his offered hand, she barely put any effort forth as he hoisted her onto her feet and steadied her, reminding her again how tall he was. "What are you, a quarterback?"

"Offensive lineman. Guess you don't come to the games."

"Not lately." Or ever, but if she'd known this was what was hiding under those helmets she might have had more school spirit.

"That's a shame."

"Well, I was planning on going to the next game. When is it again?"

He laughed. "Season's over, champ. We're just helping coach with the JV tryouts for next year."

She was an idiot. "Oh. I guess I'm more of a baseball girl."

His mouth hooked into a half grin as his gaze softened, dark lashes feathering over deep brown irises. "What's your name?"

Those eyes. They were hypnotic. "Katherine McCullough."

Recognition flashed in his gaze. "Is your brother Luke McCullough?"

"He's one of my brothers. I have five."

"*Five?* Holy shit."

"You know Luke?"

"Anyone who follows the game knows your brother. He's incredible. He'll have a scholarship to play ball before he's a junior if he keeps at it."

Luke loved football in a fanatical sense, which was probably why she didn't follow the sport. When the living room was dominated by every national and college game and draft pick, and the dinner conversation centered on drawn out debates over plays and coaches, it seemed impossible to stomach another minute of sports talk. But she hadn't realized he was *that* notable of a player for a varsity offensive whatever you call it to know his name. Now she really felt terrible for not following the school games more closely.

So she didn't sound like a total moron, she said, "He's always loved the game."

Ant grinned and glanced at the clock by the scoreboard. "So where are you rushing off to, Katherine?"

"I, uh…nowhere."

"If you give me five minutes I can give you a lift home."

Her eyes widened at his unexpected offer. "Oh, no. That's okay. I…" *Have complications.* "…have a boyfriend." *Sort of.*

His smile faltered, but he quickly recovered. "My mistake." He hesitated a moment. "Well, it was nice…bumping into you."

"Ditto." She winced as she heard how corny her response sounded. She'd definitely watched the movie *Ghost* too many times since it came out a few years back.

Staring at her a moment longer, he nodded and disappeared into the guy's locker room. Collecting her belongings, she stepped aside as a rush of beautiful young women filtered into the gym. Kate sighed as the stereo blasted and the cheerleaders fell into a well-practiced routine. When she made it to the parking lot, Nick's car was gone.

The following day she waited for Nick at his locker as the last bell rang, but he didn't show. When ten minutes passed and the halls were empty, she gave up.

That night she called him, but his mom said he was out with friends. It was pretty surprising how easily he could disappear in a small town. The following night was the same. By Thursday, she was highly irritated. It was one thing to just blow her off, but she needed to talk to him and she'd told his mother to tell him it was important three times.

Friday afternoon, she ditched the last five minutes of

sixth period and waited in the parking lot by his car, determined to catch him before the weekend. Students anxiously pulled away from the school and the east field filled with athletes as she scanned for him. *Finally,* after about twenty minutes of standing in the sun, she saw him walking toward the lot—with Cheryl. Grinding her teeth, she silently counted to ten.

"Hey...Kate," he greeted, putting some distance between him and her ex-best friend. Cheryl looked at the ground as if they were total strangers.

She'd deal with her later. Addressing Nick, she said, "I've been trying to get ahold of you all week."

He palmed the back of his neck and flushed. "Yeah, my mom said you called. I've been busy."

"I can see that. Can we talk? Privately?"

"Uh..." He glanced at Cheryl. "We were going to head into town—"

"It's important. I'm sure Cheryl can meet you there." Her friend looked up and Kate mentally dared her to object. This was serious and if she were any sort of friend she'd know that. But she wasn't her friend and she'd never be her friend again.

"Sure." He turned and sent Cheryl an apologetic glance, but she was clearly pissed. Rolling her eyes, Cheryl pivoted and walked toward the school. Nick turned and faced Kate. "What's up?"

Oh God... she'd been so focused on finding him, she'd hardly thought about what she might actually say. Collecting her thoughts, she blew out a breath. "Um..."

She looked for a place to sit, but other than in his car—the place that got her into this mess—there was nowhere to rest. She leaned against the hood and hissed as the sunbaked metal scorched her thigh.

Shocked at how awkward this all seemed, she fidgeted. It wasn't like she had much time to prepare. She peed on a stick and three minutes later—*boom*—pregnant. She was still processing.

"Kate?"

"I…" This was going to change his life as much as it would change hers. She actually took pity on him and hated the fact that she felt responsible for the unwelcome news about to hit him, even though this was both of their faults.

Just say it! "I'm pregnant, Nick."

His brows shot up. "What?"

God, it felt good to tell someone. "I'm pregnant," she repeated. Now that all the cards were on the table they could work on their plan. It was such a relief to have someone share the burden.

"Since when?"

"I'm guessing since last month." There hadn't been anyone before him.

"Jeeze, Kate." His cheeks flushed as he blew out a heavy breath. "What are you gonna do?"

She frowned as the word *you* heaped all the responsibility right back into her lap. "I figured the first thing to do was tell the father." Then they should probably let their parents know, because there was no way they were hiding this or affording it on their own.

He looked at her and paused. "Me?" He laughed. "It's not *mine*."

Gaping at him she took a moment to fathom that he was actually trying to deny the paternity. "Nick, it can *only* be yours."

"How do I know that?"

"Because it's *yours*," she said plainly.

"That's impossible. We used a condom. I think you need to find the real dad."

Oh, her Irish shot right up. Unprepared for such denial and certain as hell this wasn't the second coming of Christ, her mother's voice came rushing out of her in a way she'd never experienced before.

"Are you out of your ever loving mind? Of course it's yours! It was you pokin' at me four weeks ago and there hasn't been anyone since—though I can't say the same for you. Now, are you gonna be a man about this or not, because what I need is a man. This *baby* needs a man, because it's gonna be needin' a father in about eight months."

Holy shit. She'd never lost her cool like that before. It was as if something triggered a maternal rage in her that had zero tolerance for bullshit. Catching her breath, she stared at him, his shock likely reflecting hers. In a calmer voice, she mumbled, "I need you to be onboard with this, Nick. We have to do this together."

Eyes wide, face pale, he stared at her as if she'd gone mad. What sort of man had sex and then acted like the only explanation for an accident was the Immaculate Conception? They had to be realistic. This was scary and she couldn't deal with it on her own.

When he still wasn't speaking she scoffed. "Well?"

"I don't know what to say," he muttered, blinking stupidly. "Are you sure? I mean, I wore a condom."

Don't freak out. She forced back her temper and calmly explained, "I took seven tests, Nick. Every single one was positive."

"Shit," he hissed, pacing away and gripping the back of his neck again. "*Shit!* This sucks, Kate. I'm going to Michigan in the fall."

A pinch of regret took hold and again she felt solely responsible for something they both caused. This wasn't her plan either. Why did her spoiled dreams seem less significant than his? Sure, she wasn't going to college, but she'd hoped to find a job and get her own place. A nursery wasn't anywhere in that plan.

Still, she apologized. "I'm sorry." She was sorry for both of them. And this hadn't been some intentional scheme to derail his life. He had to realize that.

"You're only a couple weeks. We could take you somewhere. There are places that—"

"Absolutely not, Nick. I can't do that." The sense of being cornered hit hard and she took a step back.

"No one has to know—"

"*I'll* know."

"But what about me? I don't want a kid. People have abortions, Kate. It's your right to choose."

Her hand protectively went to her stomach as her chin trembled. "I don't give a shit about what the law says. I'm not putting my mind or my body through something like that." Guilt washed over her. It did seem like the simplest solution to get them both out of a bind, but something inside of her told her that sort of decision wasn't simple at all. The emotional fall out might destroy her and she was already in a fragile state.

Though she never took a stance on the issue, those sorts of methods didn't fly in her family. They were breeders—big, Irish breeders—and if anyone ever suspected her of doing such a thing, they'd likely send her to a convent to repent—they might do that anyway. Maybe that was where she belonged.

The personal repercussions of such a decision would linger and her conscience immediately rejected that option as any sort of solution at all. She'd never survive that, especially if it were a secret she had to bear for the rest of her life.

Her vision blurred and she suddenly wanted her mother with a fierceness she hadn't felt since childhood. Though Nick was right there with her, she'd never felt so alone. Maybe she could tell her mother and it wouldn't be all that bad. They could plan a baby shower with the aunts and knit booties and paint half her room pink or blue.

Oh, come on, Kate!

Her mother was a devoted Catholic. There was no way she'd see any solution other than forcing a marriage between her and the town playboy. There'd be talk of baptisms and meetings with priests and Kate would be branded for the rest of her life once she jumped through all the hoops it would take to find a respectable position in her family's eyes again.

Her stomach hurt. Why couldn't the uncomfortable stuff be over? She'd made a mistake and didn't need anyone driving the point home. Yes, she'd need help, but mostly financially and only until she found a job, which she still planned to do right after graduation. She had a plan. Sort of. But the idea of repeating her plan over and over again for the next nine months while others judged her and questioned her irresponsibleness left her winded before the explanations even left her mouth.

Maybe it would be easier to just marry Nick, pretend they were in love, and that this wasn't such a big mistake. But he didn't want a marriage any more than he wanted a child.

She looked at him, not feeling the attraction she felt in the months leading up to this moment. God, she didn't want to marry him either—not that it was on the table. But even if it was she couldn't do it. She couldn't imagine a future with him no matter how hard she tried. Maybe she'd be a single mum and he'd be the sort of father that split the holidays and took the baby every other weekend.

A tear fell from her lashes. She was on her own. Her life would be forever changed. She loved her siblings and, as the oldest, she was well practiced at feedings and diapers, but this was different. This was *her* baby and she was terrified.

Why had she pulled away from her family? They were once her everything. She was in such a rush to break away from the chaos, she never thought about all the emotional securities she'd given up.

They wouldn't turn their backs on her like Nick. They wouldn't betray her like Cheryl. Sure, they'd be disappointed, but they'd support her once the shock faded. It had to eventually fade, right? She had to make things right at home again. Enough with the selfish teenage antics and only pulling her weight enough to get by without getting grounded. She needed to grow up.

"Kate, are you listening?"

She shook her head and realized Nick had been talking for quite some time. "I'm sorry. What were you saying?"

"There's a place right in the next county. My buddy had to take his girl there last spring. It's an in and out procedure."

Her temper returned, more resolute than ever before. "I said *no*, Nick."

"Why not? You're being selfish!" he snapped. "It would be over in a day. That doesn't seem like a lot to ask when you're asking me to change the rest of my life!"

A chill chased up her spine as her anger fled and something deceptively calm took its place. "I'm not asking you for anything."

"You're asking me for *everything*!" He slashed his arm in the air, his voice rising. "I get that you don't have any plans, but I do! And having a baby ain't part of them."

"Katherine?"

Startled, she spun and gasped as her brother took a slow step forward, his blue eyes sharp with concern. "Colin—" She choked on her panic. "What are you doing here?"

"I heard you arguing. Is everything all right?" His scowl hardened as he glared at Nick.

Colin was only a year younger than her, but he'd always been more mature than her. Knowing he'd heard them arguing, didn't bode well. "Everything's fine, Colin," she assured with false calm.

Keeping his glare on Nick, he took a slow step forward and Nick treaded back a pace. "You sure? Because it sounded quite the opposite from over there."

"We're fine," Nick said, cheeks reddened.

"I don't remember asking you," Colin snapped and softened his expression as he looked back to her.

She'd never heard her brother speak in a threatening tone. *Ever.* He was not the intimidating sort. But he *was* a McCullough and she supposed all of them had their moments. He was overdue for a freak out.

Figuring she'd better reassure him, she took her brother's arm. "I'm fine. Come on. Let's go home."

Nick held Colin's stare but couldn't match the menacing look in her brother's eyes. She tugged his arm again. "I wanna go home, Colin."

He took a step back and glanced at her, his gaze briefly dropping to her stomach. He draped a protective arm over her shoulders, but before he took another step, he turned to Nick and hissed, "Stay away from my family."

Maybe he didn't hear everything. Maybe he just saw his sister in a hostile situation and didn't like it. Either way, she was grateful for the rescue.

As he walked her to her Beretta, he continued to scowl. The uncertainty was excruciating. If he overheard, she had to make sure he kept his mouth shut. Everyone would find out eventually, but she wanted to be the one to tell them.

When he lingered at her car door, she couldn't bear his silence anymore. "Just say whatever's on your mind, Colin."

He glanced toward the field. Nick was gone, but he stared as if he were still there. "Is it true?"

Her shoulders sagged. This was the first turn of the page, the start of the many unpredictable chapters to follow. Lowering her gaze, she whispered, "Yes."

He sighed. "Kate…"

"Please don't judge me. I didn't do anything that half the school hasn't done."

A deep V formed between his dark brows resembling their father in so many ways. "I'm not judging you."

"Well, don't pity me either."

"Oh, come on, Kate. Even I know this isn't something you wanted—at least not yet."

Her jaw stiffened as her vision blurred. "It may not be something I *asked for*, but I will want this child as much as any child can be wanted, Colin. There are plenty of unplanned blessings in this world."

"I know you will. I'm just…" He shook his head and

she had no doubt he wanted to remind her of the church's stance on many things.

She couldn't bear the lecture. "I'm keeping it. And I'm not getting married."

He drew back, a look of revulsion twisting his face. "I'll be damned if I let you tie your life to that prick. You don't need him, Kate. You have us."

His acceptance was so unexpected and so needed, she lost it. Looking up at him, her face pinched as tears fell unchecked. "I love you, Colin. You have no idea how much I needed to hear that right now."

"Hey." He pulled her into his arms and hugged her tight. Colin had always seemed like a pillar of strength, never battling the trials of adolescence the way she had. Somehow he'd weathered all the awkwardness of high school, his focus on the end goal resolute and assured, and she needed his strength now.

"It's okay. We're here for you, Kate. You know that. That's what family is. It'll all work out. Don't cry over him."

She wiped the back of her hand over her cheeks and nodded. Pulling herself together. "Sorry. I've been really emotional these past few days. I'm under a lot of stress."

He nodded. "When will you tell Mum and Dad?"

Colin was always upfront and it was no surprise he'd want to unburden this secret he'd unintentionally borrowed as soon as possible. "When I'm ready."

He nodded again. "If you need me to be there with you, I will."

Wind caught a lock of her red hair and brought it whipping across her cheek. She'd do her best to break the news as soon as she came to terms with it herself, but certain things, like Nick's role in all this, would remain private.

"No one knows about Nick, Colin. I'd rather save my son or daughter the chance of ever feeling unwanted. Do you understand?"

"I understand, but Mum and Dad know you've been hanging out with him."

"I'll lie if I have to. You know how old fashioned they can be. I don't want him involved when he clearly doesn't want to be."

"You know I won't lie, Kate, but I'll keep your secret as long as no one asks."

Accepting his conditions, she nodded. "Thanks, Col."

CHAPTER 3

"You're quiet tonight, dear."

Kate turned her gaze from the evening news to her mother, finding it difficult to formulate a response over the tumultuous thoughts running through her mind and the fatigue that never seemed to ease.

"Perhaps you should head to bed. You look tired."

She was tired. Exhausted really. Her father snored from the recliner on the other end of the den and all of her siblings were upstairs. She looked at her mother, really looked at her and gave her due credit for how easily she seemed to manage so much.

"Did you ever regret marrying Daddy, Mum?"

Her mother laughed. "Now what sort of question is that, Katherine? Of course I've regretted it. I regret it every time I break my back scooping up his dirty drawers from the floor, every time I have to lug the garbage to the edge of the drive, and I've regretted it all seven times I squeezed a human being from my loins while he grinned like a bloody peacock sucking on a fat cigar—like the hard part was over."

Her mother sighed and smiled at her father with aged adoration. His belly rose under his red flannel shirt with each breath. "But at the end of the day I love the bastard anyway, so I suppose you could say my stupidity outweighs my commonsense."

She smiled, loving her mother for always being exactly who she was. "Was it really that bad, squeezing us out?"

"Some worse than others. I still haven't forgiven the twins. Your sister was no treat either. And Kelly…don't get me started. You and Braydon were my easiest." She grinned and patted her knee. "But you don't worry about that. You have years to think about other things before you need to concern yourself with those trials."

Her chest tightened and she wanted so much to tell her then and there, but something held her back. There was such innocence inside her mother at times. She feared the shock might crush that part of her forever. "Well, for what it's worth… I'm sorry we put you through any pain."

"You were the first, dear. That makes you the easiest to forgive because I wanted you with every beat of my heart. But I'll take that apology and remind you of it some day when you're rushin' off to be with your friends and forget I'm the one who brought you into this world."

Kate laughed, having no doubt she'd add that information to her artillery of maternal guilt launchers. "I think I'll go to bed."

"Goodnight, dearie. I'll see you in the morning."

That night Kate cried until she fell asleep. In the morning, she didn't feel her best and by the time she made it to school she debated going to class or turning around and driving home. It had been two weeks and Nick acted as if he'd never met her, truly abiding her brother's command to stay away.

A hand knocked on her car window and she jumped, startled as a wide smile beamed at her through the glass. "Mornin', Katherine."

She rolled down the window and the burst of fresh air steadied her nerves. "Ant. You startled me." Damn, when did air start smelling so good? She wanted to hang her head out the window like a dog.

"I like to catch you off guard. Keep you on your toes. You're late."

Her hands tightened on the steering wheel as sharp and precise panic cut into her. How did he know she was late? "What?"

He tipped his chin at the school. "First period started twenty minutes ago."

Oh, late for class. She quickly hid her embarrassment with a shaky smile. She was losing her mind, thinking some guy might know her cycle. She needed to pull herself together. "I'm not feeling well."

"Your eye looks better."

She frowned, her brain had obviously checked out for the day. "My eye?"

He pointed to his cheek. "Where I bumped into you."

"Oh. It never bruised."

He frowned. "Are you okay? You seem sort of out of it."

"I'm fine." She was getting tired of saying that. As a matter of fact, she was getting tired of everything.

Sick to death of all the irrelevant bullshit she had to attend to while her world was secretly crumbling, she laughed, the sound slightly hysterical and unbalanced. "Actually, I'm not fine. I don't know what I am." But her humor was short lived and the fragile laugh shifted into a sharp sob she couldn't hold back.

"Hey…" The car door opened and he crouched beside her. "What's going on?"

"I can't…" She could barely form words as her breath caught on a hiccupped sob. "Jesus, I'm a mess. You can go." This was so embarrassing, but she couldn't stop herself from crying. She had no control over *anything* in her life at the moment and it was mortifying.

"I'm not leaving you like this." Concern riddled his handsome eyes.

She was such a selfish person for wanting him to stay. "You don't even know me." Humiliated that she was losing it in front of a perfect stranger, she tried to pull herself together and failed. This was so silly. She'd run into him a few weeks ago and here she was having a breakdown in front of him.

"So let's get to know each other. Talk to me."

"I can't. I can't talk to anyone."

His brow pinched and she had to look away. *Why don't I have napkins in my car?*

"Is this about your boyfriend?"

She snorted, absolutely disgusted that she was once dumb enough to loan such a title to Nick. "No." She wiped her eyes on the heel of her palm. She needed a fucking tissue! "I'm sorry. I don't mean to fall apart like this. My emotions are a mess."

"Sometimes getting it out helps."

"I don't know you," she repeated, searching for anything to blow her nose in. "You shouldn't have to see this." Why would anyone want to get to know a basket case?

"Sure, you do. I'm Ant. The guy who occasionally knocks you over and mispronounces words."

A soggy laugh broke through her tears as his words registered, stilling her search.

"There's a smile."

Shaking her head, she blotted her cheeks on her shirt. "Gah! I'm a disaster."

"Maybe in that bag on the floor." He pointed and waited silently as she searched the bag for napkins. Finally she found a leftover one from Burger King.

Once she blew her nose and let out a long breath, she gave him a shaky smile. "I'm better now." *I hope.*

He cocked his head, dark brunette hair falling to the side. "You wanna get out of here?"

She should go to class or home, but she'd much rather

disappear, fall off the grid for a while. The timing of his offer was perfect and beyond tempting. But she never skipped class and knowing her, she'd get caught. Still, she played along with the idea, pushing reality back another minute or two. "And go where?"

"I know a place. We could take your car or mine. What do you say? This day needs a reset and I know just the place to find one."

Plenty of her friends skipped school, but they also had sex with no repercussions. Her luck was MIA at the moment. "What if we get caught?"

His grin widened. "No one will find us where we're going. It's quiet. No one knows about it but me."

Intrigued, she arched a brow. "Is that so?" She was pretty certain she knew all of Center County like the back of her hand, but maybe he knew a secret place the rest of them hadn't found yet.

"You'll love this place. It's awesome."

Did it really matter if she got caught at this point? Nothing would compare to the bomb preparing to drop, so she might as well take the escape he offered. She smirked, sold. "Okay, but you better get in. Mr. Capaldi's coming toward us."

He glanced at the school and spotted the teacher then shot her a panicked look. "Move over."

Laughing at his sudden alarm, she climbed over the center console and fell into the passenger seat as he squeezed behind the wheel.

"Hey!" the gym teacher called, doubling his pace.

"How the hell do you adjust the seat?"

Mr. Capaldi was running toward them so she shouted, "Just go!"

He overturned the engine then threw the car into reverse and backed out of the spot leaving Mr. Capaldi flailing in a cloud of dust. "He totally recognized me. I'll probably get written up."

"Don't jocks get a pass for things like that?"

He snorted. "Hardly."

She pivoted in her seat to watch the school shrink in the distance. Once they were on their way, she faced the windshield and grinned, feeling like a weight had already been lifted. "So where is this mysterious place you speak of?"

"Not far. You'll love it."

She watched him, hunched behind the steering wheel of her car and found it hard not to laugh. "How would you know what I love?"

Sending her a sidelong glance, he pulled to the side of the road. "I can just tell. You seem like a cool chick." He searched between his bunched up knees. "Seriously, how the hell do I adjust the seat? My knees are almost through the dashboard."

He was taller than most guys in their grade, bulkier, but incredibly lean from sports she supposed. Leaning over, she pulled the lever under the wheel and he groaned in relief as the seat rolled back. "You're too tall."

He put the car back in drive. "Maybe you're just short."

As they drove, she expected to see some remarkable

back roads she didn't recognize, but he took her right down Main Street, past the church, and down the same boring lanes she traveled every day. Pursing her lips, she said, "You sure this is a secret place? I don't see anything special yet."

"You will. Just wait a minute."

"I don't know how to *wade* a minute," she mocked his accent.

He rolled his eyes. "Relentless. Do you make fun of kids when they have a speech impediment?"

She scoffed. "You *do not* have an impediment. If you did I wouldn't tease you. What you have is a lazy tongue."

He arched a brow and glanced at her, those dark eyes catching and tugging on something deep inside of her. "I've never been accused of that before. As a matter of fact, I'm pretty sure I could disprove that accusation in under five minutes."

"Ew." She laughed, denying all flares of curiosity bubbling inside of her.

He waggled his brows. "You brought it up."

"I wasn't talking about *that*." She frowned as he turned the car directly onto McCullough land. "Um, what are we doing here?"

"It's on the way to the secret spot. Road's a little bumpy up ahead."

"This is private property."

"Says who?"

They were literally trespassing on her family's land. "The people who own it. There are signs everywhere."

"I don't see any signs."

"Right there!" She pointed.

He smirked. "Do you really think someone's going to tell the owners? No one's around for miles. Trust me. We're safe."

Hiding a smirk, she faced the windshield. The only thing up this path was the falls, which truly was one of the prettiest places in Center County, but it was sort of amusing he thought he was the only person who knew it existed. If he paid attention, he'd find her initials carved into at least ten trees along the creek.

"So how did you discover this secret place?" she asked, only mildly concerned that they might be spotted this deep in the woods. No one ever came up this way during the week.

He pulled off the main road, onto a dirt path and slowed his speed. "I was running at the park and took a little detour."

She snickered. "So you got lost." He wouldn't be the first person to get lost on their mountain. It was enormous.

"No, lost implies I couldn't find my way back."

There was something about him that was different. Perhaps it was that he wasn't from around here or maybe it was his funny way of speaking, but whatever the reason, she found him refreshing and a nice distraction from her life. He had an amusing disposition.

"Here we are." He edged the car to the side of the road. "Can you swim?" He put the car in park.

"Yes, but I don't have a suit with me."

"You might change your mind when you see the water."

She giggled. "What's *wuder?*"

"Water," he repeated, mispronouncing it again. "Stop makin' fun of the way I talk." *Tawk.*

"Sorry." But she wasn't really. His accent teetered on adorable the longer she listened to him. "Say water again."

"Shut up." He laughed and shut off the car. There was a nip in the air as the trees shaded them from the sun. The doors slammed and she held back, waiting for him to lead the way since this was his adventure and she was playing the novice.

"Check it out," he called, waiting for her to catch up.

She followed him through the brush toward the babbling brook, knowing if they stayed west the creek led to a deep quarry and stunning falls. "It's beautiful."

It was. She'd always loved playing in the falls while growing up. Somehow she'd forgotten such an escape existed right in her backyard. She hadn't been there in almost two summers.

As they pushed through branches the mouth of the creek yawned and the prattling trickle of water changed to a soothing rush. "Bet you didn't know anything like this was around here."

She smirked again. "It *is* pretty hidden." Being that it was tucked away on private property and all.

"The best part's just ahead."

They followed the dirt path and she smiled when they

reached the falls. Ant's expression was priceless and she wasn't sure she'd ever be able to tell him the truth that she'd grown up swimming in these quarries.

He kicked off his shoes and touched his toe to the water. "It's not too cold. What do you think?" His words tumbled together, *do you* sounding more like *dya.* She liked it.

"I think this is exactly the place I needed to be today."

His grin widened and he startled her by pulling off his shirt in one quick motion. Wow. Football sure did a body good. He emptied his pockets and tossed some items on his shirt where it lay in a patch of pine needles.

"You coming?"

"It's a little cold." Forcing her attention to the water seemed the only way to stop ogling him, but even as she faced the falls her lashes lowered and she glanced back. Wow.

"Once you're in, you'll adjust. Come on. It'll be fun."

She considered her clothes. She could keep her shorts on, but her shirt would be sopping wet and take way too long to dry. "I don't have a suit."

"So? Neither do I."

"You're a guy."

He arched his brow. "I'm glad you noticed."

Dear God. Those looks he came up with, they weren't the expressions of a boy any more than that body belonged to a child. He was devastating in a mature sense she couldn't quite fathom. Spotting the dark tuft of hair under his thickly muscled arms was her undoing and she forced herself to, once again, look away.

Stepping closer to the edge, he drew in a breath and bolted toward the banks, propelling off the ground and piercing the surface of water with the ease of a seal. As he returned to the top he let out startled squeal. "God, that's freaking cold!"

"Told you."

Swimming to the deep center, he smiled, his black hair slicked back like a pelt. "Come on. I won't look." He turned and faced the falls, as he bobbed in place, every swish of his arms sending a ripple of sinew through his broad shoulders.

Her debate only lasted a moment. Stripping off her shirt, wearing only her red bra and shorts, she left her shoes and clothes next to his, but didn't go to the bank. Rather, she followed the beaten path through the rocks and pulled her weight upward, catching her balance on the tree trunks as she hiked the steep hill. When she reached the top of the cliff, Ant was only a small head poking out of the surface below.

"You coming? I'm not peeking. I swear," he yelled, assuming she was still behind him.

Finding the vines where they'd hung for years, she grabbed hold of the thickest one, eased back, and ran to the edge of the cliff. Her feet left the earth and she screamed as her body went into a free fall plummeting toward the water below.

The jolt of cold shocked her system, sending her deep,

yet her toes never touched down. Her muscles tightened as her legs kicked, shooting her toward the surface. When she came up, she gasped for air, laughing, certain she'd surprised him.

"Holy shit! Where did you come from?"

Brushing her sopping hair out of her face she pointed to the vine above. "I figure if you're gonna go in, go all in."

He laughed and swam toward her, treading water just a foot away. "I knew you were a cool chick, Katherine McCullough."

Her ego needed those words more than he knew. Chances were this was the last time she'd be in any position to go flinging herself off cliffs. Soon she'd be in her mother's shoes, worrying that the vines were too dangerous and the quarries too deep.

"Thanks." His gaze held her as she smiled and her stomach jolted. Shifting her eyes toward the bank, she said, "You really don't know who owns this place?"

He'd been living in Center County since the fall. Being that everyone knew her family, it surprised her he didn't know this was their land. It also made him all the more appealing, because that meant he knew absolutely nothing about her. With him, she could be anyone.

"I thought it was part of the park, like a reserve or something. I fish here and no one's ever stopped me."

He was such a blank slate. She smirked. "Poaching from the land? You're lucky you didn't get shot."

He laughed, not seeming too concerned. "Show me how you jumped off."

About to lead him out of the water, she hesitated. "I don't have a shirt on."

He glanced at her chest, which was somewhat camouflaged by the water. "That's the same as a bathing suit."

She supposed it was close enough. Swimming to the edge, she hoisted herself onto the bank and led him up the rock path. Her body prickled with goose bumps as the breeze chilled her skin and her nipples tightened—a bit more noticeable than if she were in a swimsuit. But Ant kept his gaze averted.

He examined each vine and considered the drop. Giving the vine a tug, he glanced back at her. "I don't know if this'll hold me. You're a lot lighter than I am."

If those branches could hold her uncles he shouldn't have a problem. "It'll hold." She folded her arms over her chest to hide her breasts, unsure why each glance made her more aware of her exposed skin.

Settling on a thick, green rope he stepped back and raced forward. His yodel cut off the moment he plunged into the water. Kate laughed and followed suit. They swam until their fingers were pruned and their lips were blue. It turned into such a spectacular day she didn't want it to end.

Climbing onto the bank, he lent her a hand and hoisted her out of the water. Self-conscious, she reached for her shirt and draped it over her wet chest while she wrung out her hair.

"Your hair's really pretty. It's not a normal shade of red."

Once again, he was watching her. Not leering, but definitely looking closer than most. "Thanks."

His gaze dropped to her calves and her toes curled into the grass. Returning his gaze to hers, he smirked. "Are you one hundred percent Irish?"

"Yup. Stick me in the sun and my skin will get just as red as my hair." She glanced at his dark arms, noting no noticeable tan lines. "With a name like Anthony, I'm guessing you're Italian. What's your last name?"

"McGregor."

She gaped at him. "No, it's not."

He laughed. "Nah. It's Marcelli. Anthony Vincenzo Marcelli the third."

"Yup, that's Italian. Are you Catholic?"

Pressing his face into his shirt he tipped his head sent her a sidelong glance, hinting that he could be a sinner as much as a saint. "Yeah, but I haven't been to church in a while. I might have some repenting to do." His mouth hooked in an unabashed half grin. "I peeked."

She shoved him. "You swore!"

Laughing, he snapped his fingers in the air with feigned remorse. "Damn. I guess I lied. That's two sins."

"That'll be two Hail Marys and one Our Father," she teased.

"Worth it." He snickered. "How about you? Are you one of those good Catholic girls?"

Not by a long shot, but he didn't need to know all that. "I think my mother had us baptized in the womb. My family's super Catholic, like, if you miss church on Sunday you better be prepared to miss dinner too."

"Damn. My family's not all that bad."

She smiled. "It's not so bad, just an hour each week. My brother…he gives a lot more. I think he's going to be a priest."

His brows shot up. "Really? Which brother? Not Luke."

She snorted. "God, no! My brother Colin. He's a year younger than us."

"I never met anyone our age actually considering priesthood. Priests just sort of appear and I always assumed they're transplanted from Europe or Boston."

"Boston?"

He shrugged, the roll of his broad shoulders stealing her attention. "There's some heavy faith in Boston."

He had such a plain explanation for everything. "I guess."

Her amusement faded as she was reminded of how her family's convictions would play into her situation now that she was pregnant. Shoving her worry away, she asked, "What time is it? It has to be almost lunch."

He had one of those waterproof sport watches on his wrist. "It's almost noon. Are you hungry?"

She was starving. "I don't have any food with me."

"We could go to lunch somewhere."

"Our clothes are wet!"

"So we'll hit a drive through. Or…" He leaned forward, crossing his arms over his knees as he smiled. The dusting of hair along his forearms seemed bleached from the sun.

"There's this pub in town that makes great sliders. We could get something from there. They do takeout. You wouldn't even have to get out of the car."

"You mean O'Malley's?"

"Yeah. You know it?"

"We can't go there. My aunt owns it."

"No way."

"Way. How about we drive to a diner on the other side of town?"

The thick curl of his laughter seemed to stroke the softest sides of her belly. "Are you afraid the truant officer will catch us?"

"No. I'm eighteen. I'm allowed to leave school." It was her family she worried about. "But I have a lot of relatives and not a single one would hesitate to call my mother if they saw me out of school during the day."

"One of those families." He continued to smile at her, his gaze shifting but never fully leaving her. The wind stilled, replaced by the heavy press of his gaze, as he looked right into her eyes.

Breaking the stare, she glanced at her knees, but that didn't slow the jittery nerves dancing in her stomach. "So…" her mind flailed as she searched for a distraction as his acute attention weighed heavily on her.

"You're blushing."

No doubt. His attention burned her, heating her blood deep within and sending tingles to the surface of her skin. "It's the sun," she lied.

"Is it?" His voice was low, seemingly closer.

From the corner of her eye she saw him ease closer and her heart galloped into a fast canter. "Ant—"

"I think you're really pretty, Katherine."

Her heart thundered erratically as she searched for something to say, but nothing came. The moment stretched and the energy surrounding them tightened, thick and tempting.

His shadow passed over her as he brushed the hair away from her face, sending a sharp shiver dancing down her spine as heat bloomed thick in her belly. His breath fanned over her cheek as he eased closer.

Warm breath feathered over her skin. "Why won't you look at me?"

"Oh God." He made her so nervous she could hardly breath. Purposefully, she pulled away, shaking the drops of lake water from her hair, needing to put some distance between them before she did something incredibly stupid again.

He laughed nervously, his expression unsure. "Problem?"

She couldn't do this. Scrambling to her feet she stood and pulled her shirt over her head. "We should probably get going before someone catches us here."

Ant's brow creased with what she assumed was confusion, but he didn't object. Standing, he gathered his belongings and pulled on his shirt. Needing to feel in control, Kate returned to the driver's side of the car and adjusted the seat. Once they were on the main road she turned on some music, taking a moment to think, because she really wished she could go back in time and let him kiss her, no matter how dumb that made her.

What was she doing? She had Nick's baby inside of her. She couldn't kiss Ant! And if he knew she was pregnant he'd probably run away screaming. She didn't expect to like him the way she did, but when he looked at her everything inside of her wanted to give in and see what might happen.

Oh, God…what if she never got kissed again once the baby was born? She should have just let him do it—one for the road and all that. Damn it. Why had she pulled away? It was a stupid kiss! Not a marriage proposal.

"Uh, Katherine…the speed limit's twenty-five. You're going about fifty."

Glancing at the gauge she cursed and eased her foot off the gas.

"Are you okay?"

"Hmm? Yes, I'm fine." Her eyes remained glued to the road.

"Is it because of your boyfriend?"

She rolled her eyes. "What boyfriend?"

"The one you said you had."

Grimacing seemed less crazy, so she pinched her lips tight and held back a screech of frustration. There was no point lying. "We broke up."

"Then…is it me?"

"No, it's definitely not you." She eased her foot off the pedal a bit more. "It's me. I can't…" How should she put it?

"My life's really confusing right now. If you knew what was going on you wouldn't try to kiss me."

"Why? What's going on?"

"I'm—" She wasn't actually considering telling him, was she? She couldn't do that. She didn't know him well enough. And she didn't need rumors spreading. Her family didn't even know. Ant seemed like a great guy, but he wasn't the person she should be talking to about this. "I can't tell you."

"Russian spy?"

Her face scrunched as she glanced at him. "What?"

"Witness protection program?"

She chuckled. "Nothing that organized."

"Gay?"

She laughed. "No."

"Still in love with the ex?"

"Definitely not."

"Betrothed?"

"What is this, the seventeen hundreds?"

"You only have a few days to live?" He paused then twisted in his seat to face her. "If that's the case I think you should toss away any restraint and go hog wild. I'd be happy to help."

She laughed again. "I hope I have more than a few days to live." She'd see once she told her parents the truth.

"Pregnant?"

The car nearly swerved off the road and she gaped at him, but he laughed.

"Come on, just tell me. I'll keep your secret."

Hiding her shock, she gripped the wheel. "Why do you care?"

"Because I like you." His eyes were so charismatic and his smile so charming, she found it really difficult to deny him.

And for some reason that simple confession made her incredibly sad. She wished she'd never slept with Nick. What if Ant was the guy she was supposed to be with and now she couldn't because she was pregnant with someone else's child? Guilt ransacked her insides, as she tried to deny her regret. It wasn't that she had anything against the baby. But it did complicate the natural progression of life and that filled her with a good deal of remorse.

Casually resting a hand on her belly, she mentally apologized to the baby and tried not to think like that anymore. Regrets would only make the road ahead that much rougher. And it was a road Ant didn't deserve to be stranded on.

Accepting she couldn't lead him on, she shoved away her feelings for him and whispered, "Don't like me, Ant. You're a great guy, but I think you'd be much happier liking someone else."

"But I can't. You see, I have this copper bowtie and my heart's set on wearing it to prom. Problem is, no girl wants to wear a copper dress. But that bowtie would match your hair perfectly."

She rolled her eyes. "You do not have a copper bowtie."

"I guess you'll never know."

Seeing the diner up ahead, she debated if lunch was a

good idea. She needed to eat and she couldn't go home with wet shorts, but she really didn't want to give him the wrong impression.

"I like you too, but only as a friend." What a total lie. "Can friendship be enough?" She really needed a friend at the moment, being that her ex-best friend had permanently lost her trust and she wasn't ready to talk to her family.

"We can be friends." His grin was forced, not reaching his eyes the way it normally did and making her want to take back everything she just said.

She forced a grin as well and offered an olive branch. "My friends call me Kate."

He tipped his head to the side. "Kate. Katie. I like that."

And she loved hearing him say her name, but her disappointment was inescapable. It would be so easy to give in and not think about the consequences, but there were always consequences. Always. He was gorgeous and funny and amusing to be around, but she had to start thinking ahead. Not thinking ahead was what got her where she was and now her life was moving in a very unexpected direction.

The diner was slightly crowded with the lunch rush, but the customers were mostly truckers passing through. As they sat in a booth by the back window and perused the menus, she tried not to imagine what being with a guy like Ant might entail. He was so different from Nick. With Nick, she had to compete for his attention and do things she wouldn't normally do just to retain it. Ant seemed totally focused on her. He complimented things like her hair and called her a cool chick. She wasn't sure anyone ever used such words to describe her before and she liked that being a cool chick had nothing to do with her appearance and everything to do with her personality. It made the compliment more genuine.

Stop thinking about it!

She turned her attention to the menu. Diner menus always overwhelmed her. She could order anything from a holiday feast to breakfast to dessert, all for fewer than ten dollars. Maybe food could be her new thing.

"Coffee?" the waitress greeted, holding an insulated pot at her hip.

Coffee sounded great, but pregnant women weren't supposed to overdo it on caffeine. "I'll just have water—and a glass of apple juice, please." She hadn't had apple juice in years, but as she caught sight of an old man sipping some her taste buds seemed to do the hustle.

"And for you?"

Ant ordered a cola and they went back to looking at the menus. "What're you gettin'?"

"I'm not sure. Everything sounds good and I'm suddenly ravenous. I could order this whole menu." Pregnancy had definitely made her appreciate food in a new way.

"Get whatever you want. It's my treat."

"I have money." Besides, this wasn't a date. They were just friends.

The waitress returned and she settled on a three-cheese omelet and a side of scrapple. Ant also ordered scrapple, but paired his with a turkey club.

"You know, they don't make scrapple in other places," he said.

"They don't?"

He shook his head. "Nope. It's a Pennsylvania thing. Most people are disgusted by it."

"Well, I'm not. I love it."

"Do you know what it is?"

His dark eyes teased so she glanced at the placemat. "Yes. I don't care. People eat hot dogs. They're just as gross."

Laughing, he flipped through the beer menu tucked by the ketchup and sugar packets. "Do you drink?"

They'd never get served here. "Not lately." Or for the next eight months.

"I'm not a big drinker, but I do like a beer now and then. Can you get served at O'Malley's?"

"It depends which aunt's working."

The conversation sort of teetered out, but Ant kept it going. "So, Katie, what do you have planned for the fall?"

She could only imagine. "I've been trying to get a job working at my dad's lumberyard."

His gaze dropped to her shoulders and he smirked. "You'd look cute in flannel and a wool cap. How are you with an ax?"

"I can hold my own, but I'd be working in the office. He has a secretary, so it would mostly be light filing and stuff like that."

"No college?"

Funny, she'd always wanted to take a year to work before committing to a career path or a degree, but now it sort of felt like she was being robbed of the second half of her plan. "Not right away. Maybe in a few years, but I'll probably go local and commute."

He nodded. "I'm going to Penn State."

"Wow, really?"

He grinned, obviously proud. "I have a scholarship for housing, but I don't know if I'll take it. As much as I'd like to leave the nest, my mom does my laundry and cooks like she's feeding an army at every meal."

"You should take it. Will you be playing football then?"

"Believe it or not, it's an academic scholarship."

Oh boy...cute and smart. "What major did you choose?"

"Biobehavioral Health."

Her eyes widened and she laughed nervously. "I don't even know what that is."

"It basically focuses on solving the problems of human health and illness."

"You're going to be a doctor?" He was definitely out of her league.

"No, it has more to do with epidemiology. Research for disease control and environmental issues."

Her body sank a bit deeper into the booth. Here she thought he was just a carefree jock, but then he went and pulled out his big, fancy future and turned out to have a crap load of potential. He'd be off studying to save the world from the next plague or possibly working to cure cancer and she'd be trapped in this little redneck town, living in her childhood bedroom, raising a fatherless child, likely working at her father's lumberyard during the day and renting out shoes at the local bowling alley at night.

"What's the matter?"

She picked up her juice and drank from the straw. "Nothing. You're a little intimidating, that's all."

"I wasn't telling you that to make you feel bad. I think it's cool you're taking some time to figure out what you want to do. My dad went to Penn State, so it's sort of been drilled into me since childhood. Believe me, I'd much rather blow off the next year and figure out who I really am."

But she wasn't blowing it off. She'd be working and saving every penny she made and even now she knew that would never be enough to actually get ahead, not with another mouth to feed.

The waitress delivered their food, but Kate's appetite had dwindled. Ant didn't talk much as he devoured his sandwich, but when he was finished he said, "Do you think I could talk to your dad about giving me a job this summer?"

She lowered her fork. "You want to work at the lumberyard?" Didn't he ever take time off to just kick back?

He shrugged. "It would be better than being trapped in some office all summer. No offense."

If she actually did get the filing job and he worked at the yard, they might still run into each other after graduation. That made her happy, being that once he started college their paths would go in polar opposite directions and they'd probably never see each other again. "I can ask him."

"I can give you a copy of my resume. I don't want it to seem like I'm asking for a hand out. I'm a good worker. In Philly I worked at a sausage factory."

She grinned. "You made sausage?"

"Yeah. If you want, one day I'll make you some—from scratch. The trick is stuffing it with broccoli rabe and asiago cheese. Once you taste it you'll never be able to eat the over processed stuff again. Maybe we can make it together. I'll give you my secret recipe."

She couldn't imagine meat stuffed with vegetables and cheese, but she wanted to try it. "Okay. I'd love that."

"How about this weekend? Do you have plans?"

Plans? *Ha!* "No, I'm free."

"Perfect. I'll pick you up Saturday morning."

"Morning? Are we making breakfast sausage?"

He laughed. "No, but it's an all-day process. We have to go to the market to get everything fresh, grind down the meat, tenderize it, stuff it. It's a long day, but it's fun."

Another chance to escape. "I can't wait."

That afternoon, she drove him back to school just as the last bell rang. As students trickled out of the building Ant hesitated. "I had a great time today, Katie."

She liked when he called her Katie. Most people didn't.

Just her parents and her siblings on occasion. "Me too. Thanks for showing me your secret spot."

His full lips curved in a half grin. "Any time."

"Well…" She patted her fingers on the steering wheel. "I guess I'll see you Saturday."

"Or maybe I'll see you in school tomorrow."

Duh. "Yeah, or that."

He continued to stare at her and her gaze bounced nervously around the limited space, but it was hard not to look into his tempting gaze. His door cracked open and she shut her eyes, her breath clogging in her throat, as the pain behind her ribs tightened. She wasn't ready to see him go.

"I'll talk to you soon. Oh—" He paused and her lungs tightened another degree. "I almost forgot. I need directions to your house for Saturday."

"Um…" She detailed the way to her property and he frowned.

"You live right by the falls."

Her cheeks heated. "My family sort of owns the mountain."

His lips parted as his eyes closed and he shook his head slowly. "Well, don't I feel like an idiot."

"Don't. I loved that you brought me there. It was such a nice day—perfect really."

"Please don't tell your parents I was trespassing. It wouldn't look good during my job interview."

She grinned. "Your secret's safe with me."

CHAPTER 4

"You seem quite chipper today, Kate. Did you have a good day at school?" her mother asked as they peeled potatoes at the sink.

She stilled, realizing it was the first time in weeks she'd been in a good mood. "It's just a nice day."

"Feels good now that this weather's warmer. Hopefully we get to enjoy spring before summer hits and I'm drippin' sweat from my nickers."

She laughed, because her mother never mastered the feminine grace of other moms. As she thought about how mopey she'd been and how attuned her mother was to her moods, her gaze lowered. "I'm sorry I've been in a mood lately, Mum."

"Oh, we all have our bouts. No use apologizing. You'll be moody again soon enough."

Kate looked at her, wondering why she'd say such a thing and what she was implying. "What do you mean?"

She rinsed the potato skins out of the sink. "Just that you're a woman and we all have our moments." Her work-roughened hands carried the strainer full of spuds to the cutting board by the stove.

Maybe Kate was making too much out of a little accident. Sometimes her mother could be incredibly understanding. "Mum…can I talk to you?"

"I swear to Lucifer himself, if your father doesn't fix this burner soon I'm going to stop cooking." She hit the center of the stove with a rolling pin and clicked the knob a few more times. "*Frank!* The burners out again!" Abandoning the stove, she grabbed a stack of plates and went about setting the table. "What did you want to talk about, love?"

Her father came in and fiddled with the burner. "Maureen," he snapped. "How many times do I have to tell you hittin' the thing with a rolling pin isn't going to fix it? It's the valve."

"You're lucky I don't take the rolling pin to your head. Just fix the damn thing and shut your gob." She grabbed a handful of napkins and carried them to the table. "What were you saying, Katherine?"

"Nothing," Kate murmured, her courage gone. "I'll get the silverware."

There was always too much going on in the house. Someone was either interrupting or they were talking about something totally unrelated to Kate's issues, making it impossible to shift topics.

After dinner she went to her room and decided to

clean out some things she no longer used, because somehow purging her physical items seemed the most cathartic action she could handle at the moment. But deep down she wanted to unload the emotional.

By the time she was finished sorting out her clothes, half her drawers were empty and the stuff that remained wouldn't fit in a few months. She bagged up the salvageable items to take to GoodWill. Maybe she'd find some maternity clothes while she was there.

There was a knock at the door and she shoved the bag in the corner as her mother entered, carrying an armful of towels. "Well, is it my birthday? I don't recall your room being this clean since the day your father finished the floors."

"It needed it."

Her mother smirked and sat on the bed, casually adjusting the pillows the way they should probably be. "You want to tell me what's been on your mind, dearie? At first I thought it was just girl talk, but now I'm wondering if you have a guilty conscience."

Shit. Here was her opening, but she'd lost her nerve. "It's nothing."

"Oh, come now." She put aside the towels and pulled Kate to sit beside her and rubbed her hands affectionately. "Is it a boy? Are you in love?"

"God, Mum, no." If only her problems were that simple.

Leaning close, she nudged her shoulder and whispered, "You can talk to me, Kate. I know I'm older, but I remember what it was to be young." She lovingly tucked a strand of hair behind Kate's ear. "You'll be graduating soon enough and I'll miss these chances to talk with you once you've moved into your own place."

Her head lowered as pressure built in the back of her neck. "I'm not sure if moving out is the right thing to do anymore."

"Because of work? You'll find a job, love. Did you talk to Daddy?"

"Not yet."

"Do you want me to start nagging him for you?"

She chuckled, knowing just how relentless her mother's nagging could be. "That's okay. I'll ask him."

Her mother nodded. "Well, if it helps, I'll butter him up with a nice pie for you. Not that I think you need help. He'd give you the moon if you asked it of him."

Biting her lip, she tried to breathe through the crushing guilt in her chest. It was true, her parents would do anything for her. They'd suffer anything to make any one of their children's lives easier. Knowing how disappointed they'd be in her broke her heart. They'd worked hard to make sure she had a decent future lined up, but now her direction swerved and there was no getting back to the path she'd been traveling.

She couldn't bear all the worrying another minute, her shoulders literally trembling under the pressure to unburden herself. "Oh, Mum...I messed up." A tear fell, making a dark splotch on her jeans.

"It can't be all that bad, Katherine. Tell me what's wrong and we'll figure it out together."

"It's bad. I don't want to tell you."

Her mother tsked. "You're a good girl, love. I'm sure it's not as bad as it seems."

Wiping her eyes, she battled to get the words out, clutching every excuse to prolong disappointing her parents. "You'll be upset and I don't want you to be."

"Is it drugs?" her mother asked, her tone shifting into something serious. "Are you takin' the pot, love?"

She laughed and sniffled. "No, I'm not 'taking the pot'. Where did you even hear that term?"

"I watch television." She nudged her again, pulling her close in a sideways hug. "You know nothing you tell me will ever make me love you less, Katherine. You're my baby and I'll always protect you as best I can. Now, tell me what's got you so upset lately. I can tell something's been weighing on you."

She shut her eyes, because somehow that made her words easier to manage. "I'm..." Her stomach twisted so tight she could barely breathe. "I'm pregnant, Mum. I'm sorry. I'm *so* sorry. I didn't mean for this to happen and I swear we were safe, but... I'm just so sorry."

When her mother remained silent, Kate wiped her eyes and forced herself to face her. Her expression was blank, but she saw the confusion in her eyes. "Please say something, Mum."

She licked her lips and looked at the floor. "Well... I wasn't expectin' that." She shook her head. "For Christ's sake, Katherine. You're not even married," she said, hardly speaking above a whisper. "Who is the father?"

"Mum," She silently pleaded for her too look at her, but her mother's head remained angled away. "No one waits for marriage anymore."

"Well, I sure as hell did," she scoffed. "Not only are you a McCullough, you've got O'Leahey in your blood. You can't share a toilet seat with a man without gettin' pregnant. What on earth were you thinkin'?"

Though she wasn't yelling, just sort of thinking out loud as she processed the news, Kate wished she could take her confession back. "I was thinking we were safe."

"How on earth did you even buy…" Her head shook as she frowned. "My God, I don't know what the kids call prophylactics these days. Your father always handled that and, as you can see, he was rather lax in that department."

She couldn't handle a speech about her parents' sex life. "I swear we used a condom, Mum."

Her mother sighed, grooves taking deep shape in her brow where lines of worry might forever stay. "Was…was this the first time?"

Kate nodded.

"Oh, dear…you *are* my daughter. I suppose if you plant an onion you get an onion." Her head rolled back and she drew in a long breath. "You're father…"

"Please don't tell him yet. I swear I'll tell him, but I'm not ready yet."

Her lips twisted. "How far are you, love?"

"Six weeks. Almost seven."

She folded her hands in her lap. "Well, that's not too bad. Summer's coming. Your aunts and I could throw something together by August and I can make you something that hides your belly. We'll have to talk to his parents and have a sit down with the Father Mark. He is Catholic, isn't he? We'll be wanting a proper ceremony—"

Fear choked her as her mother barreled in the exact direction Kate hoped to avoid. "No, Mum. There isn't going to be a wedding."

Her body stiffened. "What the bloody hell do you mean there isn't going to be a wedding?" And there was her mother's Irish temper, stealing the air right out of the room until Kate's lungs felt the pinch.

Her mother's wild green eyes met hers, as she hissed, "Katherine Mary McCullough, my first grandchild is not going to be a... a... Well, it's just not! Now, you want me to keep this from your father, that's fine. I'll hold my tongue for a few days so you can get your affairs in order, but I'm telling you right now, if you think he's going to let some scoundrel just walk away and leave his little girl in a mess, you don't know a thing about the man who raised you."

"Mum, I can't make someone do something he doesn't want to do."

She snorted. "You don't know the first thing about men, love. That's all marriage is!"

"I'm not marrying anyone!" Kate snapped. Her mother was living in a nineteen fifties fantasy world. "People don't have shotgun weddings anymore."

"Well, your father still has a rifle, so we'll see about that. Now, you listen to me. You talk to this boy tomorrow and bring him here for dinner. I'll want to meet him—"

"No, Mum! That's not how this is going to work." Even if she begged, Nick wouldn't willingly come to her house. And she refused to beg him for anything.

Startled, her mother stood. "Now, listen here, Katherine. I might be long-winded, short tempered, and out of style, but I know a thing or two about raising children and I know your father. I'm not telling you what you can do. I'm letting you know what *he will* do. I've watched that man walk away from plenty of nonsense, but this is not a joke. He is not going to stand idly by while some boy gets a pass after doing this to his daughter. You think I have anything to do with that? I couldn't stop him if I tried. Frank is his own person when it comes to those he loves and he loves you fiercely. So much so, that boy had better know what's coming for him if he isn't here to meet your father and break the news himself."

Kate's stomach sank as she turned away from her mother, truly regretting that she'd opened her mouth. There was no way she'd convince Nick to meet her parents. And after the past two weeks, she didn't want him to. "What if there's no father involved?"

"Oh, well, let's round up the three kings and clean out the manger!" she cried, almost hysterically. "What do you think this is, the second coming? Of course there's a father and the minute *your father* finds out who he is, he'll be dragging him to the church by his face."

"Mum, Daddy can't just threaten him—"

"Have you met your father, Katherine? That man does whatever he pleases and doesn't go around checkin' to see if he's within the law."

"You can talk to him—"

She held up her hands. "You told me to keep my mouth shut. Now you want me to soften him up?"

"A minute ago you were offering to make him pies!"

"That was when I thought you were takin' the pot!"

"Stop saying that! No one says that!"

"Takin' the pot! Takin' the pot!" she yelled, like a senseless child having a tantrum. "You're sittin' here tellin' me how to talk when you've got bigger issues to deal with. Sweet Jesus, Katherine, what about your future? Are you positive you're not just late? Perhaps you have the bloats."

"It's not gas, Mum!" Kate shouted and suddenly they both fell silent.

Her mother's face tipped forward as she shook her head. Kate's heart raced, as tears stained her cheeks, unsure how they'd gone from a heart to heart to a screaming match. A hiccupped breath left her mother's lips as her shoulders shook.

Kate hesitated, as her mother pressed her palm over her eyes. The unbearable pain of watching her mother cry was more than she could handle. "I'm sorry I screamed at you, Mum."

Her head fell back and she hooted and cackled, startling Kate. She took a hasty step back, seriously worried about her mother's sanity.

"And here I thought you were bringing home a bad grade. I never saw this coming." She met Kate's gaze. "Where the hell are we gonna put it? We're burstin' at the seams here!" More disbelieving laughter. "Oh, it'll be wonderful. We'll cram a crib into the corner and use the old John Deere as a stroller." She hooted and bent forward, catching her breath. "Christ, I need a drink." Then she snorted. "I'm bettin' you do too, but there'll be none of that. Not for the next few months at least. Trust me, you'll make up for lost time once the baby's here."

Kate frowned. "Are you all right, Mum?"

She wiped the tears from her eyes, which seemed a mixture of sorrow and delirium. "I'm fine, dear. Just taken a little off guard, but I'll adjust. It's not the first time I've been surprised by a pregnancy."

She was an absolute lunatic, of that Kate was sure. "Are you going to tell Daddy?"

"*Hell no!* I'll make him a pie and hide his bullets, but that's the best I can do." Another clipped burble of laughter slipped out. "I'll warn you, though. He's a resourceful man when he wants to be. I once saw him take out a rabid skunk with nothin' but a rock and a bandana."

This was not the reaction she'd been expecting. "Are you mad at me?"

"What?" Her mother's humor fled as she took her hands and leveled her with a serious look. "Oh, darling, no. I mean, I'm surprised. We're going to have to shift some things around, maybe move your brothers out to the barn, but I'm not mad at you." She smiled. "Babies are blessings, even the unexpected ones. I know this is scary, but we'll get through it. Everything will work out in time."

Despite knowing her mother was delusional, her confidence helped. "I'm sorry I won't be able to move out for a while."

"Pish. If we turned your room into a gym I'd never use it anyway."

Kate chuckled and rested her head on her mother's shoulder. "I love you, Mum."

She patted her cheek and hummed. "I love you too."

CHAPTER 5

"*A*ren't you going out tonight?"

Kate stilled as her father's question interrupted the show she was watching. "Um, I don't feel like going anywhere. There's nothing going on."

"What do you mean? Finn and Luke said there's some sort of fair going on at the park."

"Dad, Finn and Luke are in junior high. We don't hang in the same circles."

He held up his hands in defense. "My mistake. I just figured you'd want to be with people your own age."

"Are you trying to get rid of me?"

He chuckled. "Maybe. Your sister, Braydon and Kelly are at Aunt Colleen's for the night. I figured your mother and I might have some privacy."

Realizing that she'd interrupted some elderly love fest she scrunched her nose. "Ew. Dad, don't tell me things like that."

"You asked."

"Asked what?" her mother said, coming into the den and taking up the other side of the couch.

"Nothing."

"Katie's staying in tonight," her father explained, implying her presence threw a wrench in his plans.

"Oh, well, that's fine," her mother covered. "It's nice to have quality time."

"Yes," her father grumbled. "It is."

When no one paid attention to him, he sighed and took the remote. Her mother sent her a commiserating wink and Kate smiled. They watched a terrible movie with lots of explosions and her father fell asleep. They tried to change the channel, but every time anyone touched the remote he woke up and demanded he was still watching, only to fall asleep again in the next minute.

Kate started dozing off around nine when headlights flashed in the window, signaling someone was home.

"That might be Paulie dropping off the kids. I sure hope he remembered to bring back my cookie sheets Colleen borrowed. I swear that woman's entire kitchen is stocked with things of mine she's never returned."

The door opened and Finn came in with a wide grin. "You're up. Good. We found something at the fair for you."

"For me?" Kate turned a thumb at her chest. "I hope it's funnel cake."

Her brother laughed. "He's getting out of the car."

"He?" Kate asked, confused.

"He?" her mother echoed, perking up.

"Yeah, he gave us a ride back."

A nervous pulse started in Kate's chest as she sat up. "Who?"

Her mother was already off the couch and looking out the window. "Oh, he's tall." She glanced over her shoulder. "Katherine, fix your hair."

Kate scowled. "No."

Her mother tsked and bustled toward the kitchen. "I'll make some coffee."

As soon as they were alone, Kate hissed at Finn, "What did you do?"

"What?" he shrugged. "Luke knows him and he said you two were friends."

Wait. What? That didn't sound like Nick. She shook her head. "Who is it?"

"You'll see. By the way, I saw Nick making out with two different girls tonight. Stay away from that guy, Kate."

Wonderful. "I plan to."

Luke stepped through the door and everything inside of her seemed to lift on a deep breath as she recognized Ant's dark hair.

"Wow, this place is awesome. Hey, Kate." He nodded and she wondered if his greeting was so casual because her brothers were watching.

It didn't matter. She was thrilled to see him. "Hey." She stood and tossed the blanket on the couch, frowning at her baggy sweatpants and flannel shirt. That was fine though, because friends saw each other like that. "What are you doing here?"

"I ran into Luke and asked what you were doing. He said you were in some sort of woman funk so I said we should go cheer you up. The fair was lame anyway."

Great. I'm a charity case. "I'm not in a funk."

"Then why weren't you at the fair?" he challenged, a playful glint in his eye. "They had Dippin' Dots."

"If only I'd known," she teased with mock regard.

"Yeah. I was gonna grab you some, but I couldn't decide what flavor to get and the line was really long. But maybe tomorrow we can get some. Fair's here until Sunday."

"Oh! You should go, Katie!" Her mother barreled into the conversation, smiling brightly up at Ant. "I'm Maureen, Katherine's mum. Her favorite flavor's strawberry, by the way."

"Mum!" Kate snapped. She couldn't go to the fair, because that would be too much like a date. "Sorry," she apologized to Ant, but he just kept smiling.

"It's nice to meet you, Mrs. McCullough. Your home's beautiful."

Her mother preened. "Thank you. Katie's told me so much about you."

Kate's smile faltered. "What—"

"Katherine, the coffee's probably ready."

Anxious to get him away from her mother, she grabbed his arm. "Come on." Her mother lingered in the hall, probably asking Luke and Finn what Ant's name was being that she'd *heard so much about him!*

"Your mom seems nice."

"Nice like a jack in the box. Give her time. Eventually she'll make you want to scream."

He laughed. "What?"

"Nothing. Do you want coffee?" She grabbed two mugs from the cabinet, returning one as she recalled she couldn't have caffeine.

"Hey, are you upset I'm here? I can go."

She turned and sighed. She loved that he was there, but…her family…they were a little overbearing and high-handed on most days. "No. You don't need to leave. I just wasn't expecting visitors."

He took a step toward her, but then hesitated. She had the sense that he would have moved closer if something hadn't stopped him. Vulnerability flashed in his dark eyes as his grin softened. "I…missed you."

Oh God. She turned and filled his mug. "How do you take your coffee?"

"Cream and sugar."

Her hands shook as she poured the cream. His proximity pressed into her like a full body caress even though they weren't close enough to touch.

"I can't stop thinking about you, Katie."

"Shit." Coffee dribbled down the mug as she over poured. "What's that?" Of course she heard him, but she needed to stall in order to think up a proper response. Once she had the mess wiped up, she turned to find a spoon and stilled.

He looked into her eyes, blocking her path to the

drawer, all humor gone. His skin was utterly flawless. She swallowed thickly. "I need a spoon."

He took a step closer and she backed up, her butt bumping into the counter. "I couldn't wait until tomorrow to see you."

They were making sausage together. She hadn't forgotten, but now, looking into his eyes as her heart pounded erratically just from being close to him, she wasn't sure that was such a great idea. Several garbled sounds left her throat, the only one that made sense was the repeated, "Spoon."

He leaned closer and she sucked in a breath, his scent creeping to the very depths of her. Her stomach flipped nervously as she feared and, against her better advice, *hoped* he'd kiss her. How could something so wrong seem so right? Why did she have to like him so much? She needed a friend and keeping him as one meant keeping her stupid crush to herself.

The drawer to her left slid open and he held up a fork. "We keep ours next to the sink too," he whispered, the full pillow of his lower lip seeming to curve around each sylla-ble. She wanted to lick it. Clearly his heart wasn't about to beat out of his chest the way hers seemed ready to do, because he could still manage words.

She licked her lips and tried to get her act together. "That's a fork," she rasped, still leaning back as he was too close for her to catch her breath. God, he smelled incredi-ble. Not that cheap stuff everyone else wore. His scent was unique, maybe not even from a bottle. Just...good.

He reached behind her again, rummaging through the drawer and pulled out a spoon. "I guess it's only proper to spoon before we fork."

"Okay!" she sang, spinning out from between his hard body and the counter. *Is it hot in here?* Being a total ninny, she did the only thing she knew would keep his flirty ass away, something she'd surely regret. "Mum, you want a cup?"

Her mother came into the kitchen wearing a smile suited for Christmas morning. "I'd love one." She collected Ant's arm and bustled him to the table. "So, Anthony, tell me about yourself."

"Um… I go to school with your daughter. Know your son from football. And I'm hoping to apply for a job working for your husband this summer."

"Oh," her mother twittered like this was the best plan in the world.

So help her, she'd never hear the end of it if the woman found out about his plans to be a bio-whatever doctor with his fancy scholarship to Penn State.

"Katie's also plannin' on workin' there this summer. You two could have lunch dates."

"Mum."

"Cream and sugar, dear. You know how I take it. Now, where is that accent of yours from? New York?"

"Philly."

Her mother hummed. "Philadelphia. We went there once. They wouldn't let me ring the Liberty Bell. I'm loud, so I like loud things."

Ant laughed. "So is my family."

Her mom laughed. "Oh, we know what that's like, don't we Katherine? We're all loud. Do you have a big family?"

"Three sisters. I'm the oldest."

Her mother's eyes widened as her smile grew. She was totally seduced by him. "And how long have you known Kate?"

"We met—"

"Mum, drink your coffee before it gets cold."

Her mother obediently sipped. "This will keep me up all night. I should have made decaf."

Inviting her into the kitchen was a mistake. "Do you want to sit out front and talk?"

"Sure." He sucked down the last of his coffee and followed her through the screen door.

Once she was on the porch, she let out a long breath. "Sorry. I think my mother worked for the CIA in a past life. She loves interrogating people."

"No problem." He looked around the dark yard. "Hey, is that a tire swing?"

"Um, yeah."

"Awesome." He bounded down the steps, his long legs carrying him with the grace of a wild gazelle, and she slowly followed.

"Haven't you ever seen a tire swing before?"

He hopped on the large tractor tire and pushed off the trunk of the tree. "No. There aren't a lot of big trees in the city. Your house is amazing, like a real log cabin. You must love living here."

She frowned. "How much sugar have you had tonight?"

His foot dragged over the ground as he brought the tire to a stop. "A little. I'm just happy to see you. Get on."

"We both won't fit."

"Sure we will." He glanced up at the ropes and gave them a tug. "Here…" He pulled his legs out of the hole and stood on the side of the tire, holding his balance with the riggings. "I'll help you up."

Glancing back at the house, she sighed. Where the hell were her brothers? She needed buffers. "It's really meant for one person at a time."

"Oh, come on. Don't be a chicken."

She rolled her eyes. "What are you, five?"

He blinked those big brown eyes. "Please."

Pathetic. But she couldn't resist him. She reached for the rope and hoisted herself up. The tire spun as her weight was off balance with his. Her feet shifted and she reconsidered how safe this actually was. "We're gonna tip."

"No we won't. I got you."

His hands closed over hers and she shut her eyes, letting the heat of his fingers seep into her skin. She wouldn't be able to hold onto her resolve if he kept touching her like that. "Ant—"

"Don't make another excuse, Katie. I know you feel this thing between us."

Her chest lifted as she drew in one deep breath after

another. Breathing only pulled his scent deeper, not clearing her head at all. *Focus!* "That's not the point."

"So you admit it?"

Her eyes opened. Another mistake. His face rested along the center rope, only two inches from hers. She instinctively leaned back and his hand tightened over hers.

"Careful."

Trapped, she looked back at the house. "I thought we were going to be friends."

"I am your friend."

"This doesn't feel like friends," she whispered, hating how much she wanted to lean into him and press her lips to his.

His breath teased her cheek, his voice a soft rumble that teased her insides. "What does it feel like?"

Amazing. Butterflies. Roller coasters. Strawberry ice cream. And strangely sad. "I can't be more than your friend, Anthony."

"So just be my friend."

Blinking up at the branches, she swallowed back the pain of unfair timing and forced herself to make responsible choices. "You can't look at me like that."

"Like what."

Her gaze met his and it cost her, bringing back the reality of how badly she wanted to throw caution to the wind and give in to him. "Like you're doing now."

The reflection of the moon played over his eyes,

making silver pools in his dark irises as his gaze softened. "But I like looking at you."

Her head lowered, her resolve depleting with every breath of him. "I have to get down."

"Wait—"

"No, Ant. I need my feet on the ground."

He released her fingers and she slid down the rope. When she was back on solid ground, she faced the house. "Maybe we should cancel our plans tomorrow."

"Why?" His shoes thumped on the grass as he jumped off the swing. Why did every move he made reverberate through her, emphasizing his graceful strength and gentle mannerisms? "I don't understand what the problem is."

"I...I don't like you that way." It was a lie, but she couldn't keep fighting the amazing chemistry they had, especially when he looked at her like she was somehow more special than every other girl.

"Oh."

Her lashes lifted as the ache in her chest tightened. He sounded so dejected and wounded. She couldn't possibly mean that much to him, but as his dark lashes fanned down casting shadows on his cheeks, she recognized his disappointment. "I'm sorry. Right now just—"

"It's fine." He waved a hand. "I just assumed..." He laughed to himself, doing a poor job at playing off his frustration. "Sorry. I thought we both felt something."

"Anthony—"

"It's cool. I get it." He glanced at his watch. "I should probably get going."

She hated seeing him like this. He stopped looking at her and now he was leaving. "Please don't be mad at me."

He laughed, but it wasn't his usual laugh. This one sounded hollow and forced. "Why would I be mad at you? We're friends, right?"

"Right," she said with little certainty. "Are we still hanging out tomorrow?" She wasn't sure why she asked, because whatever his answer, she'd be sad. If he said yes, it would be awkward. If he said no, it meant they'd probably never be normal around each other again.

"Sure."

"You don't sound like you want to anymore." Sad it was. But perhaps that was for the best. "It's okay if you don't."

"What do *you* want, Kate?" His eyes flashed in the shadows as they narrowed, pegging her in place. "I thought we had plans. If you changed your mind, just say so."

She didn't like the challenging tone in his voice. Stiffening her shoulders, she met his glare. "I planned on making sausage."

His brow tightened as if he were getting some rush from an argument that only flustered her. "Then we're gonna make some sausage."

Her mouth tightened. "Good."

"Fine," he snapped. "I'll pick you up at ten."

"I'll be ready." She shoved her hands on her hips.

Glaring at her, his broad shoulders slowly pumped with each breath. His firm lips softened as his mouth hooked into a grin and his eyes creased. "Damn," he whispered, biting his full lower lip. "I bet you have one hell of an Irish temper."

Her heart fluttered as his glare shifted into such an intense stare she trembled. He looked at her like he wanted to eat her alive. He could never know how deeply he affected her.

Laughing nervously, she threatened, "Let's hope you never see it."

His mouth held in a cocky grin. "Let's hope I do. I'll see you in the morning." He turned and swaggered off to his car like he'd just won half a battle.

As he drove away a sense of depletion stole over her. It was getting more and more difficult to combat his flirting. Even arguing with him seemed more like foreplay than anything else. Stepping into the kitchen, she paused as Luke looked up from the fridge.

"Hey." He went back to nosing through the leftovers. "Ant leave?"

"Yeah." Should she tell him not to bring him here anymore? Would that even solve anything?

Luke stood and guzzled milk from the carton. "Ant's a cool guy. You got something going on with him?"

She frowned. When she'd been dating Nick, Luke never made a comment, yet he seemed to almost encourage her relationship with Ant. "No. We're just friends."

He laughed, his brow creasing as if she weren't making sense. "He likes you, Kate."

"We're just friends." How many times would she have to repeat that before it started sinking in?

Luke shook his head, tucking the milk carton back in the fridge. "You're nuts. He's way nicer than that other dipshit you were hanging with. Why do girls always go for the assholes?"

"I don't go for assholes, Luke." Nick technically wasn't an asshole until after they broke up.

"Whatever, I'm just saying you can do better than some jerk who hooks up with your friends. Ant's a good guy and you should give him a chance."

"I don't like him that way."

He scoffed and rolled his eyes. "I'll never understand girls. Suit yourself. I'm going to bed."

She stared after him, wondering when he'd stopped being a kid and started acting like one of her peers. Though she'd always been closest with Colin, the older her other brothers got, the more she realized they'd eventually all catch up to one another. Once again she felt guilty for not taking more of an interest in Luke's life.

"Luke?" she caught him before he made it up the stairs. "Yeah?"

Blinking at him, she saw so much of her father in his stature and strength, no longer the little boy he'd always been. "Did you make the team?"

He grinned. "Yeah. Why?"

She shrugged. "I heard people talking about how great you are. I just thought you should know. Congratulations."

His smile doubled. "Thanks, Kate."

"Let me know when your first game is and I'll be there."

His brow lifted, giving away a bit of his surprise. "Yeah? That'd be great. I'll let you know."

"Goodnight."

He stared a moment longer and nodded. Though Luke wasn't as congenial as Finn, they were both great guys. She decided to take some time to get to know them better, find out who they really were aside from being her little brothers. Suddenly, her relationships with her siblings seemed crucial and precious in a way they hadn't before.

She shut off the kitchen lights and took the stairs. Maybe if she invested more time in her family, the other relationships in her life wouldn't feel so overwhelming.

CHAPTER 6

Ant pulled up to the log cabin at nine fifty-seven and debated if he should beep or knock or what. He didn't have the chance to decide as Katie came bounding out of the house in a flash of red hair looking prettier than… Well, she was probably the hottest girl he'd met since moving here. And she was going to spend the whole day with him.

He got out of the car and grabbed her door. Something told him Kate was the sort of girl that deserved to have doors opened for her. "Hey," he greeted and she smiled.

"Hey." She had the prettiest eyes. Sometimes they looked green, but they were mostly blue.

As he closed her door and rounded the car, he reminded himself to play it cool. So far, he'd struck out every time he tried to get close to her. He didn't want to piss her off and he definitely didn't want to overestimate his chances, but something in his gut told him their chemistry was mutual. He didn't usually respond to girls the way he responded to her and he liked it—liked her.

He climbed behind the wheel and shut his door. "So you ready to get your Italian on?" He winced. That sounded totally cheese-dick.

Her laugh was a comfort, the soft, raspy sound easing a bit of his tension. "Sure. I'm not really sure what that entails, but I'm up for the challenge. You should know, I come from a long line of fierce chefs and I have some experience with making sauce."

This was good. Talking was good. "What sort of sauce?"

"Spaghetti sauce."

He backed out of the long drive. "Oh, you mean gravy?"

"No, sauce."

"Sauce goes on a sandwich. Pasta gets gravy."

"Then why do they call it marinara sauce?"

"They don't. It's just marinara or gravy. It all depends what you put in it."

She mumbled something under her breath.

"What was that?"

"I said I know an Italian that would probably school you on sauce."

"Oh, really?" He laughed, loving her feisty side. "And who is this Italian you speak of?"

"She goes by Italian Mary and she eats little boys like you for breakfast."

"Ha! I have to meet this woman. How do you know

her?" He followed the road out of town heading where his father told him he could find some decent cuts of meat.

"She's my aunt's mother-in-law and she's right off the boat."

"I bet she calls it gravy."

"No, she doesn't," she argued, her voice taking on a whole new sexy lilt. "First of all, she barely speaks English, but I know she calls it sauce."

He relented. "Fine. But you have to introduce me to her so I can check her out."

"She's single. Want me to fix you up?"

He sent her a sidelong glance. "I like 'em Irish." When her smile trembled he quickly said, "I was joking. Relax." Okay, it was definitely too soon for that.

She glanced out the window, her deep red hair streaming down her arm like silky ribbons. "Where are we going?"

God he wanted to run his fingers through her hair. "We are going to find some grade A pork butt."

"What?"

Good. Her smile was back. "It's the main ingredient in sausage."

"What's the real name?"

"Pork butt. That's the name of it."

"No, it's not."

"Oh, okay. Jeeze, you argue a lot for a person who doesn't know the difference between gravy and sauce."

"Oh, shut up." She clicked on the radio and he grinned as his favorite CD came on.

"I like this song." He turned it up as Dave Matthew's voice filled the car. Keeping his attention on the road, he only spared her a glance every few seconds.

"*Am I right side up or upside down,*" she sang, her voice soft and melodic.

She rolled down the window and her hair flicked across the seat like the tail of a kite. The scent sank into him and his eyes nearly rolled back in his head as she pressed her face into the wind and smiled. At the end of his life, when he was old and senile, he'd probably still recall how beautiful she looked in that moment.

His body tightened and he reeled in his thoughts before he embarrassed himself. There was something about Dave Matthews Band that instantly put him in a good mood. Whipping out his best yodel, he sang, "*Lovely lady, I will treat you swee-ee-eetly.*"

She glanced at him, silently giggled, and he fell another peg. When she looked at him like that, laughed with him, it was incredibly freeing. He wanted to reach across the seat and touch her any way he could, but he resisted.

When the song ended the disk skipped to *Crash Into Me.* She didn't sing or hum this time, but he could tell she was really taking in the lyrics. He didn't know what made her look sad sometimes, but he saw it in the thoughtful turn of her eyes and the way her mouth seemed to wear all of her worries, barely holding in its secrets.

He wanted her to open up and confide in him. He wanted to know whatever she was working so hard to keep inside. Maybe then she wouldn't frown as often, because she had a mouth made for smiles and he wanted to give her as many as he could.

There was definitely something between them. It didn't seem normal to simply sit in silence and enjoy a person the way he enjoyed her, especially after only knowing each other a few weeks.

"You solving world peace over there?" he asked, and she blinked at him as if recalling his presence.

"Sorry. I was zoning out."

"It's okay. The scenery doesn't need words sometimes."

She glanced at the view, but there was nothing particularly breathtaking outside the car. "Can we listen to something else?"

"Sure," He switched off the CD and turned on the radio. "You can put on whatever you want."

She toyed with the dial for a few minutes then shut the music off completely. What changed? Did that song mean something to her? Bring back bad memories? Maybe she caught him checking her out and thought he was a creeper. Shit. He hoped that wasn't it.

"Hey, you okay?"

"Nope."

His brows shot up. He didn't expect that sort of answer. Had he pissed her off? They were fine a few minutes ago and now she seemed upset, but nothing happened. "Want to talk about it?"

"Okay."

Another surprising response. This girl was totally unpredictable.

"Tell me why guys get a pass when girls don't?"

"Uh…what do you mean?"

"I mean, they can basically do whatever they want and no one questions them. If a guy sleeps with a bunch of girls he's a hero, but a girl who does the same is a whore."

"Um…" He didn't know if this was about her or someone else. "Did someone say something about a friend of yours or something?"

"I…" She hesitated. "Have a friend."

"Okay." The friend was obviously her.

"She made a mistake. She was with a guy who had a reputation and now he's moved on, but she can't. He's already slept with other people—*her friends*—and he just acts like nothing happened when her life is flipped totally upside down."

"Did they have sex?" If someone hurt her he wanted to know who it was.

"Yes."

He tried not to wince at the thought of her being so close to another guy. "Well, was she okay with that?"

"Sort of."

His hands tightened on the wheel, but he kept his shoulders relaxed. "Kate, sex isn't a *sort of* thing. It's either consensual or it's not."

"Well, my friend was a virgin. Everything happened really fast and he never really asked."

The pink of his knuckles bleached from his skin as his grip twisted tighter. "What do you mean he didn't ask? Did you say no?"

"I'm talking about my friend."

Sure she was. "Sorry. Did she say no?"

"I…don't know. She…can't remember."

"Was she drunk or something?"

"No, but it happened after a party and she had a few drinks."

He chose his words carefully, so not to scare her. "Katherine, if someone is too drunk to make a decision, it's the same as not having a choice. Maybe your friend should report this guy so he doesn't do the same thing to someone else."

"No, it's not like that. She could have stopped him, but it was already happening and it didn't last long enough to make a big deal out of it."

This guy sounded like a selfish jerk. No surprise he couldn't last, but that wasn't the appropriate thing to say. If this actually happened to *her* that was pretty messed up. "I'm sure that wasn't how she'd imagined her first time."

She scoffed. "Definitely not."

"Well, I hope the next guy's better to her."

"I don't think there will be a next guy."

His gaze shot to hers then back to the road. "Come on, Katie. We're young. People screw up. She shouldn't let one asshole dictate her future. This guy was obviously a loser. A good guy wouldn't be like that. He'd know when she was ready and he'd *ask*."

Her head tilted and her hair hid her face. "I guess."

"Hey." He really wanted a name, but he couldn't ask her that. Unsure if touching her would piss her off, he chanced it anyway and grazed the back of his knuckle along the side of her knee. "Not all guys are assholes, Katie. And just because a girl mistakes one asshole for a decent guy, it doesn't make her a whore. It makes her human."

She tucked her hair behind her ear and nodded. "I know you're right, but I just feel… sorry for my friend. She's not having such an easy time lately."

"Is she talking to anyone?"

"Well, there's this one friend who's been helping her. He's sort of like a distraction, but…"

Shit. He was the distraction. "But he likes her?"

"Yeah."

His ethics outranked his libido and all the heat inside of him cooled. But it wasn't an easy shift, more like a fire hissing under a bucket of ice water. "Well, I'm sure if he's a good guy he'll pick up on her signals and wait until she's ready."

Her mouth twitched into what might have been a smile. "I think she likes him too, but she's just not at a place where she can date."

Fuck. All his plans for the day took a backseat, as he finally understood what she was saying. He was definitely the distraction and that was all he'd ever be to her, because some fucking douchebag screwed her over. But maybe with time, her heart would heal. He could be a friend, help her with that. "Who was he, Kate?"

She shook her head. "He's no one."

That was the truth. The guy sounded like a real no one.

It was probably best he didn't know his name. "You're right. He is a no one."

Accepting that she wasn't ready for anything more than friendship, he looked for the silver lining. They were still hanging out for the day and they were going to make sausage and maybe later he'd talk her into some strawberry ice cream at the fair. But he'd scratch the whole plan to kiss her on the Ferris wheel.

Attempting to revive her mood, he said, "If you're nice, I'll let you pick out the butt."

She chuckled. "I'm not exactly sure how to judge a pig butt."

"Judge it just like you would a human ass. It should be firm, yet tender when you grip it, and meaty enough to take a fair swat. If you need to use mine as a guide that's fine too."

She snorted. "Can I swat it?"

"Only if I can swat yours."

"Not a chance."

When they arrived at the market they made a spectacle of swatting packaged meat. Katie picked out a decent pork butt then turned into a total girl when he grabbed the tub of intestines to case the sausage.

"You've eaten sausage before. What did you think the casing was?"

"I don't know. I don't think about that stuff when I'm eating." She gagged and shoved the container away.

"Oh, stop. Irish people eat blood pudding. That's way worse."

Her lip curled and suddenly she looked a little green.

"Hey, you okay?"

Her fingers trembled to her lips and turned away. "Yeah." Goose bumps rose on her arms. "I just got a little…" She shook her head. "I think the smell of raw meat is getting to me."

He sniffed. "You can smell the meat? What are you, a vampire?"

Little beads of sweat glazed her brow. "I think I need to step outside for a minute."

"Okay. Should I come with—"

She turned and raced for the exit.

"Shit." Ditching the cart, he went after her, but she wasn't out front. "Kate?" Where the hell did she go? "Katie?"

A soft moan traveled from around the corner of the building and he went to investigate. Kate was hunched over, one hand to the wall, and a pile of puke at her feet in the grass. He didn't want to embarrass her, but he also didn't want to leave her there throwing up at the side of the building. Stepping back, he looked for a vending machine and spotted one just inside the market.

Once he bought a bottle of water, he returned out front and lingered at the corner of the building. Shit, she was really sick. He hoped she didn't have the flu. They should probably scrap the whole food plan for the day and take it easy.

She groaned and he chanced approaching. "I got you water."

"Thank you." She glanced at the grass and staggered toward the front of the building. Her coloring was off and she had a waxy sheen coating her face.

"Are you sick?"

"I didn't have breakfast."

"We don't have to go back in there. There's a McDonald's we passed on the way in."

"I don't think I can keep anything down right now." She chugged half the bottle. "I'm sorry. I've never just thrown up like that."

He shrugged. "It happens. Do you feel better now that you got it out?"

She snickered with little humor. "Oh, it's not out."

"Do you want me to take you home?"

"Can we just sit for a minute? I don't want to get sick in your car."

He nodded and led her to a bench that wasn't down wind. "I might have a granola bar in my car or something."

"Thanks, but I think I just need to sit still for a minute." Her hand rested on her stomach.

"Does your stomach hurt?"

"No."

But her hand continued to hold her flat belly as if it was unsettled. They sat in silence for a good ten minutes. It was a nice day, so he didn't mind waiting with her.

"I think I'm better now." She sighed, her lashes casting shadows on her high cheekbones as she breathed in a deep breath.

"Want to head back?"

"What about the sausage?"

He shrugged. "If you don't feel good we probably shouldn't cook today."

Her pink lips pursed as she pouted. "I really wanted to make sausage with you. I'm sorry, Ant."

He nudged her shoulder. "Hey, it's cool. We have all summer to try again."

"Before you go to school?"

"Yeah." The obstacles sure were piling up. She had baggage from whatever guy screwed her over and he was leaving for college in less than three months. Glancing at her, he debated if she was worth the effort. She twisted the empty water bottle into a ball and lobbed it at the nearby trashcan, making the shot. Yeah, she was totally worth it.

"What do you say we hit up another diner and grab breakfast?"

She smiled. "You're sure?"

"Positive."

They stopped at the same diner they ate at before. This time Kate ordered kielbasa with extra sauerkraut and hot mustard. When the waitress delivered their plates he stared at hers. "You sure that's gonna help your stomach?"

"This is exactly what my belly wants right now. Don't judge. Wanna bite?"

"No." He wasn't sure how she managed, but she devoured the whole thing. "I don't think I ever saw a girl kill a sandwich like that."

She shrugged. "I'm not a typical girl."

"No?"

"Nope. I can hit a moving target with a compound bow from over a hundred yards away and you should see me field dress a deer."

He blinked at her, unsure how to respond. One, he wasn't sure what a compound bow was and two, he never killed a living thing in his life. "You hunt?"

"Since I was thirteen. My dad started teaching my brothers when they were old enough and I wanted to do whatever they could do."

He couldn't quite picture her cutting open a deer, but he liked imagining her dressed in camo. "Do you eat the stuff you kill?"

She nodded. "I don't like hunting for sport. I think it's wrong on some level, so we always use the meat. Big family, lots of mouths to feed."

"I've never hunted."

"No? How come?"

He laughed. "They get antsy when you try to shoot things in the city."

Her smirk was patronizing in the sexiest way. "I forget you're not from around here."

"You're getting used to my accent."

"I guess I am." She sat back and patted her belly.

"You feeling better?"

She hummed happily and sighed. "The belly's happy."

Thank God, because he didn't want to cut their day short, even if they weren't cooking. "So do you have guns?"

"No. My dad does, but his are too big for me. My grandfather left my mom his old Winchester and I've used that one a few times, but I'm best with a bow." She laughed. "Why are you looking at me like that?"

"I just never heard a girl talk about guns before."

She waved a hand. "Everyone in my family knows how to shoot. It's just who we are. It's not a big deal. We keep the guns locked up most of the time."

"Can you shoot a handgun?"

"I'm sure I could, but I only use rifles for hunting. Handguns are for other things."

"So if a person broke into your home, would you shoot them?"

Her brow creased. "I don't know. We don't even lock our doors. I guess I would if I thought my life was in danger, but we don't have a lot of break-ins around here."

"Remind me to always knock when I come to your house."

She laughed. "We don't shoot people. Well, my grandfather shot my dad, but that was a different time."

"Your grandfather shot your dad?"

"Sort of. Shot *at* him. No one really knows the whole story except my aunts and my parents. I think they exaggerate."

He sat back and finished his soda. "Your family's a little nuts, huh?"

She shrugged. "Not nuts. McCullough. The longer you know us, the more normal we seem."

"Can I get you anything else?" the waitress asked as she approached.

He arched a brow and Katie asked, "Can I have a strawberry shake in a to-go cup?"

"Sure thing, hon. How about you?"

He loved that she didn't hide her appetite in front of him. "I'll take a chocolate shake." When the waitress left, he looked at Kate for a long moment. Her coloring was back to its normal shade of perfect. *God, she's pretty.* "I guess you just had a bug or something."

She shrugged. "Or something."

After their shakes were delivered and they settled the bill, which Kate refused to let him handle, they drove back to the mountain. Kate showed him the lumberyard and it was a little intimidating. This was no small operation.

"Does your dad hire people without experience?"

"Sure. You'll pick it up quick."

"Let me guess, you also know how to climb trees."

"Climb them, cut them. I was raised in the country."

"You're just a regular ol' country bumpkin."

Glancing over her shoulder, she grinned at him then hefted her feet off the ground and she swung on a low hanging branch. Adorable—and fucking hot. Her breasts jutted against her shirt and his mouth practically watered. She was totally in her comfort zone. When he thought about their earlier conversation and how unsettled she sounded, it really pissed him off, because if one thing was clear it was that Katherine McCullough didn't scare easily.

After the lumberyard they visited the park and sat on a

swing set, chatting about nothing and everything. By the time they made it back to her house she said she was tired. "It's only six o'clock." He didn't want to be a prick, but he really didn't want to say goodbye just yet.

"I know, but I haven't been sleeping much at night. I constantly have to pee."

He couldn't help but laugh. She hunted, climbed trees, knew how to handle a bow and a rifle, and talked about pee. Maybe they were too deep in the trenches of the friend zone to pull back. "We could watch a movie or something."

"Where? Here?"

He shrugged. "Maybe." He noted her hesitation and said, "If I'm inviting myself and overstepping—"

"No, we can watch a movie. But I should warn you, my house isn't really quiet. There are nine of us and it's Saturday so my grandmother's probably here."

"I don't mind noise. I'm Italian."

"Okay."

He didn't know what crazy assumption made him think Italians had the market cornered when it came to breaking the sound barrier, but he clearly underestimated the McCulloughs. They walked into an absolute clusterfuck.

Mrs. McCullough was screaming at Kate's dad and swinging a rolling pin in the air. A little girl with red hair like Kate's had a blue eyed kid pinned to the floor as she pounded the ever-loving shit out of him with her fists. Luke and Finn and another guy screamed at the television in the den while a blond kid came trampling down the steps at about a hundred miles an hour.

"So help me Jesus, if you don't fix this damn stove I'm going to let you starve! I want a sandwich, he says. Do we have anything sweet, he asks. I'm gonna give you a sweet taste of my foot when I jam it up your arse the next time you expect me to cook on a broken stove!"

Kate smiled. "You remember my mum."

Mrs. McCullough lowered the rolling pin and flushed. "Oh, hello, dearies. Did you make your sausage?"

Shaking off his shock, Ant shook his head. "No, Katie got sick."

Her mother cocked her head. "Are you better now? Did you have something to eat? You have to remember to eat, love."

"I'm fine, Mum," Kate assured, but didn't seem too happy about her mother's concern.

"You sick, Katie girl?" her father asked.

"No, I just got a little nauseous at the meat market. I was fine once we left. Dad, this is Ant. He's thinking about applying for a job at the yard this summer."

Ant's shoulders drew back as the man's stare drilled into him. He hadn't intended to talk about the job until he had his resume in order.

"That so? You ever work in a lumberyard before?"

Okay, this guy was totally intimidating, like the Bounty man on steroids with knuckles stained from hard work and forearms the size of Popeye's. He definitely knew how to use an ax. Ant took a step away from his daughter. "No, sir. But I'm a fast learner."

His blue eyes scrutinized him as his brow folded. "You from the city?"

Ant nodded. "Philadelphia. We moved here last fall."

The man glanced at his daughter and back to Ant. "You keeping company with my daughter?"

"We're just friends, Daddy."

This guy was definitely not the type that should be called *daddy.* Unless it was in the big daddy sense, like when a pack of hard ass bikers rolled up on hogs and went Thunderdome on a place. Maybe then.

His eyes narrowed as he let out a slow breath. "Come by after school on Monday and we'll see how you do."

Can I bring protection? Maybe he'd ask Kate to guard his six with her crossbow. "Thanks. That would be great."

"We're going up to my room to watch a movie," Kate announced and Ant wanted to run. Didn't she remember this guy had guns? *He totally knows you picture his daughter naked.*

"Keep that door *open,*" Mr. McCullough growled.

Great. Her father wanted to kill him and had a whole mountain to hide the body.

Tell my mom I love her.

CHAPTER 7

"I'm just going to use the bathroom real quick," Kate said as they entered her bedroom. After everything she ate and being sick that morning, all she could think about was brushing her teeth. "My DVDs are on the windowsill."

Ant nodded and she left him alone. When she returned he was still standing, but holding the empty case of *Austin Powers*. "Did you put it in?"

Ant pivoted. "What?" His eyes were uncharacteristically wide. "Oh, the movie. Yes."

Kate frowned and lowered herself to the bed. "Are you okay?"

He nodded, but seemed a little jumpy and nervous.

She scooted across the mattress so her back was against the wall and her legs could stretch out. "Are you going to sit?"

He searched the room. "I'll just sit on the floor."

She snorted. "What are you talking about? Don't be ridiculous. Sit up here." She tossed him a pillow and he held it at his waist.

Reaching for the remote, she cued up the movie. Ant didn't make his way to the bed until the opening credits were over. Once he was sitting beside her, he seemed stiff and alert. She wasn't sure what happened to make him high strung all of the sudden. He was usually so relaxed.

Being that she owned the DVD, and watched it a hundred times, her attention faded and her eyelids grew heavy. Resting her eyes for a minute, she wilted into the warmth at her side.

"Kate?"

"Hmm?" she hummed, lacking the strength to open her eyes.

"Uh…you're sort of leaning into me."

So tired. She should move. She shouldn't lie on Ant like that, but he was like a big pillow that smelled really nice. "Comfy." Her mind jerked as she fell deeper into sleep. She should sit up. "Want me to move?" He was so warm.

After a long moment, he whispered, "No."

THE MOVIE ENDED and Ant debated starting it over just so he could have more time with Kate. Beautiful Kate. Fiery Kate. Crossbow Kate. Lying on his lap with all her sexy red hair Kate. He hadn't moved a muscle in two hours except to play with the tips of her hair when he was certain she was out cold.

But now the movie was over and it was after eight. He should probably get going. Sighing, he brushed her hair behind her ear and looked at her one last time. Her cheeks were like porcelain and her lips were the deepest pink he'd ever seen. Pressing his head to the wall he silently groaned. He wanted to kiss those lips so bad, but he couldn't.

Time to go. "Katie."

"Hmm."

"The movie's over."

She stretched and his eyes went wide as her cheek nestled into his thigh, her mouth turning toward his stomach. Blinking at the ceiling he silently cursed and cleared his throat. "I should probably get going. It's late."

Slowly, she rolled to her back and stilled. Silky strands of hair trailed over her brow and neck as her eyes flicked open. A pregnant moment passed as she stared up at him, realizing she'd been sleeping with her face on his lap. Sure, he could have nudged her off, but he liked her there. Each time she nestled closer and settled a bit more, his body trembled with the hot burn of anticipation—painful, yet excruciatingly pleasant.

Maybe because he couldn't have her he wanted her all the more. The waiting was intoxicating. Addicting. Yet he couldn't wait for it to end. But she was fragile and had been hurt and needed time to get over the past. None of that led to a hookup any time soon. But tonight, as he watched her sleep and savored every press of her body into his, he realized he'd wait her out as long as it took, because there was something special about her.

"Did I fall asleep on you?"

"Yeah. I didn't mind." He loved it.

She rolled again, this time returning a platonic level of space between them. "Sorry."

He twisted his legs over the side of the bed and casually adjusted his jeans. "It's fine." His gaze shifted over his shoulder and he stilled, entranced, as she pulled her hair into a ponytail.

Her long ivory neck had a beauty mark under her left ear. The collar of her shirt was crooked and he could see the strap of her bra. Purple. The day at the lake it had been red. She didn't wear a lot of jewelry, just a leather band around her wrist and one of those Irish crown and heart bands on her finger.

"What's your ring called?"

She gave her ponytail a yank and looked at her hand. "This? It's a Claddagh."

He knew there was some code about the ring, something about the way a girl wore it that told if they were dating, single, engaged or married, but he wasn't sure exactly what meant what. "What does it mean when it's worn like that?"

She fanned out the fingers of her right hand and looked at the ring. The crown was closest to her knuckle and the heart pointed toward the tip of her finger. "Nothing. It just means I'm alone."

"What if you turned it around? Does that mean you're taken?"

"It's supposed to mean my heart's locked away from others because it belongs to someone else. You only turn it when you're in love." She glanced at her left hand. "When a girl's getting married, she wears it on the left hand and turns the crown outward after she says her vows." The fingers of her left hand balled into a fist. "Why?"

He shrugged and stood. "Just curious." Not wanting to say goodbye, he stalled. The words came out of his mouth before he truly considered what he was asking. "Do you want to come to Sunday dinner at my house?"

"Tomorrow?"

"Yeah." Holy crap, did he really just invite her to meet his family? "We eat around two."

A little V formed between her eyes. "You said dinner."

"It's how we do. You want me to pick you up?"

"Sure. Will there be sauce?"

He laughed. "Smart ass. No, but there might be gravy." If they were there, this was the moment he'd kiss her. He shifted toward the door.

"I'll let you know if there's a difference."

God, he loved what a ball breaker she was. He'd been nervous he wouldn't see her again until school on Monday, but this was much better.

As he left, he tiptoed past the den where Kate's father slept on a chair like a slumbering bear. As Ant passed the kitchen, Mrs. McCullough spotted him.

"Anthony, are you leaving?"

He stilled, glancing back with relief as Kate's dad still slept. "Kate was falling asleep."

She smirked and stepped into the hall. "You'll have that more and more, now," she whispered, taking his arm and pulling him into the kitchen. "I want you to know you're always welcome here. We'll figure things out with Frank, but I think havin' you around will help smooth matters over, you know? And gettin' you in at the yard will make him more comfortable with the situation."

A little confused, he assumed she was saying Mr. McCullough wasn't such a bad boss once a person got to know him. "Well, I hope to show him I'm dependable. I don't plan on missing a day and I hope to adjust as fast as possible."

Her smile grew as her hand tightened on his arm. "Aren't you a lovely boy? Oh, I could just weep to hear you say such words." She nodded. "My Katherine did good bringing you here."

One of the boys—the one with dark hair—came in and opened the fridge, stealing Mrs. McCullough's attention. "Kelly, I catch you drinking out of that carton again I'll sew your lips shut."

The boy turned, bright blue eyes flashing with guilt. "I didn't—"

"Don't lie to me. I bought that milk today and it's half gone. I know what cups I wash."

"Mum, it wasn't me."

Her lips pursed. "Go tell your brothers if I catch them

drinking from the carton I'm sicking your father on them." She rolled her eyes. "Bunch of animals." As the boy scurried out of the kitchen, she shouted, "This is why we can't have nice things!"

That was his cue to leave. "Thanks for having me."

She smiled, surprising him with the approval he found in her eyes. "Don't stay away too long, you hear?"

As he walked out to his car there was a skip in his step. Though he was making slow progress with Kate, her mother seemed to be a big fan of his. If he could win over her dad and get the job at the yard, which Mrs. McCullough seemed to think was in the bag, maybe Kate would finally see he wasn't such a bad guy. Today was definitely progress.

THE FOLLOWING AFTERNOON, just after the kitchen was cleaned up from breakfast, Ant's mother's voice shook the rafters. "Nicky! You expect these meatballs to roll themselves? Anthony! Let that dog out before it pisses on my carpet! I'm runnin' to the store. Lock the top lock behind me and keep your father out of the fridge. We got company tonight."

He glanced at the ceiling and waited for it.

"Anthony! This dog is pacin'! I come back to shit on my carpets, you're cleanin' it up!"

"I'll handle it, Ma!"

The door slammed. If he hadn't witnessed how loud

and crazy Kate's family was he would think twice before bringing her here, but something told him she could handle his mother. Taking the stairs two at a time, he called the dog as it circled the parlor. "Come on, Povi. You gotta go out?"

The dog followed him through the kitchen where his sisters were elbow deep in veal and pork.

"Who's comin' to dinner tonight?" his sister Nicky asked.

"You got a girl comin' over? Who is she?" Maria kicked off the interrogation.

"What girl?" Angela echoed. "Does she go to our school? Do we know her?"

He stood by the back door and waited for the dog to handle his business. "No, you don't know her and she goes to my school." His sisters all attended the Catholic school in the next town because his father believed girls needed a little more supervision during their teen years. "Did you guys give Povi those treats again? He's got the trots."

"Ma did," Angela said.

He rolled his eyes. "She bitches he's always shittin' on her carpet but she keeps feeding him those treats. Throw them away."

"*You* throw them away," Maria snapped. "We're busy makin' meatballs for your girlfriend."

"She's not my girlfriend."

His sisters snickered. "That's not what Mommy said."

Great. He opened the door and called, "Povi..." When

the dog came running, he looked back at his sisters. "Where did Ma go?"

"To pick up Nonna and get more garlic for the braciole."

The gravy was already simmering on the stove in the big pot. He lifted the lid and breathed in the savory scent. Using the wooden spoon he stole a taste. "This needs salt."

"Mommy said don't touch it."

"It needs salt," he argued, searching for the shaker.

"She said don't touch it," Angela snapped, waving him away like a housefly. "Get out a' here!"

Unable to find the salt he went in search of his dad, who was predictably washing the car out front. "Hey, Pop."

"Ah, finally some help. Grab the bucket." Ant moved the bucket closer to his dad who was polishing the headlights of his Lincoln with a toothbrush. "Your mother..." he grumbled, shaking his head, silver hair slick against the black. "She's freakin' nuts. What do I do *every* Sunday?"

Ant sat on the front step, stretching his legs across the walk. "Wash the car."

"I wash the car. All the sudden she's tellin' me I gotta go get more long hots for dinner."

He wasn't sure if Kate would eat hot Italian peppers, but if she did she probably wouldn't eat more than what they already had. "She'll be fine when she gets back, Pop. You know how she is."

He grumbled again. "Who's this girl?"

"Her name's Kate McCullough. You'd like her."

"Irish?" His head bobbed in a nod. "Good. You already got enough Italian women in your life. Don't want too many." He moved to the other headlight and mumbled. "Every day that woman gets closer and closer to my last nerve."

"We're just friends." When his dad screwed one eye shut and gave him a look like he was full of shit, Ant explained, "I'm workin' on it."

His dad laughed. "Atta boy."

His mother returned and screamed at his father for dragging the garden hose over her hosta then she moved into the kitchen where she ordered around his sisters. Ant watched television, but mostly kept his eyes on the clock, counting down the minutes until he could pick up Kate.

"Anthony," his mother interrupted his show, hovering in the parlor door. She had her stained cobblers apron on, the one that buttoned down the front. "You want a snack? How about I make you a nice sandwich? I got *capicola* at the deli."

"I'm all right, Ma."

"You sure? You look irritable. You should eat."

"I'm not hungry."

She waved a hand. "I'll make you a sandwich."

Ten minutes later he was eating a sandwich while his sisters continued to slave away in the kitchen. There were definitely some double standards in their house, but he never complained because he was the son. Modern girls didn't go for those sorts of rules, so he milked it from his mother as long as he could.

At one-thirty he decided he'd waited long enough.

"I'm going to pick up Kate," he told his mother, searching the counter for his keys. "Did someone move my keys?"

The kitchen smelled fabulous, but there was shit everywhere. He lifted cutting boards, moved bowls, and searched the table, which was covered with drying pasta.

"You mind? I'm workin' here," Maria snapped.

"Who moved my keys?"

"Say a prayer to St. Anthony," his mother suggested like she did whenever anything was lost and he rolled his eyes.

"I left them right here on the counter."

"Did your father eat this cheese?" his mother barked. "I told him it was for dinner."

Lord help him. He was never getting out of there. "Where the fuck are my keys?"

His mother slammed the fridge and turned, her eyes narrowing. "The mouth on you." She snatched his keys off the windowsill behind the sink and held them in front of his face. "Don't speed."

"I won't."

She grabbed his face and kissed his cheek, slapping him twice, but with affection. "And be a gentleman. Hold the door for her."

"I will, Ma. I gotta go."

When he made it to his car he was in a sweat. Anxious to get to Kate, he took the back roads so there would be less traffic. When he pulled up to her house there were two unfamiliar cars parked in her driveway. Thinking about the invitation her mother made the night before, he got out and knocked on the front door. Voices traveled through the open windows but no one answered the front door.

He followed the wrap around porch and the voices grew louder. When he reached a screen door to the kitchen he knocked again and the noise silenced. Three women sat at the long kitchen table staring at him. One was older, but the other two looked about Mrs. McCullough's age.

"There's a man at your door, Maureen," the blond woman said.

Mrs. McCullough came to the screen door and pushed it open. "Anthony, come in." He stepped into the kitchen, the weight of each woman's scrutinizing stare making him itch under his shirt. "This is Katherine's boyfriend, Anthony."

Not her boyfriend. "Hello." He waved and they all suddenly started talking at once.

"When did she get a boyfriend?"

"I didn't know she was dating?"

"How come you didn't tell us, Maureen?"

"That tan skin. He's no Irishman."

Startled by their unfiltered inspection, he hitched a thumb toward the hall. "Is Kate here?"

"Of course, love. *Katherine!* Anthony's here!"

He winced as Mrs. McCullough's voice pierced the sound barrier. She sure had a set of lungs. He wasn't sure who would win in a screaming match, his mother or Kate's. Hopefully, they never found out.

Kate came into the kitchen and all thoughts of mothers fled. Her hair was down and she wore a fitted tank top with a pair of jeans and a thick belt. His chest tightened as he drew in a breath, his eyes taking in every dip and curve. "You ready?"

"Yup." She tucked a thick hank of hair behind her ear, flashing a tiny green stone on her lobe. For some reason that little earring was significant. Kate didn't usually wear jewelry, but today she wore earrings. That had to mean something and he hoped it meant she wore them for him.

"Where are you off to," the blonde woman asked. "You look pretty, Katherine."

Kate flushed. "Just to dinner."

"Dinner? We just had brunch."

"It's an early dinner." Kate met him at the door. "Let's go," she whispered quickly then went to kiss the older women on the cheek.

Once they were in the car he asked, "Were they your aunts?"

"Yeah. They're a little nosy. Did they talk to you?"

He shook his head. "Not really." More like they talked *at* him.

Her hands fidgeted in her lap. He tried to think of something to say, but he was strangely nervous about bringing her to his house. Every time he drew in a breath to talk, he chickened out and stayed silent. Before he came up with anything to say they were sitting in his driveway.

Kate looked at her hands as her thumb spun the ring on her finger.

"We don't have to stay long," he said, hoping to put them both at ease.

She peeked at him from under her hair, her eyes a definite shade of blue today. God, he wanted to kiss her.

"It's fine. I just…" She glanced at his house, which was a quarter the size of hers. "Is anyone else going to be there?"

"Just my parents, my sisters, and my Nonna."

She nodded and opened the car door. He wasn't sure why this felt weird. It shouldn't, but it did. He walked her through the garage and opened the door that led directly to the kitchen. Voices shouted before anyone heard them come in and then everything went quiet.

His mother beamed and tossed the spoon on the stove. "Come in. Come in." She took both Kate's hands and led her to the table, shoving her into a seat. "I'm Anthony's mom. You can call me Loretta. These are Anthony's sisters, Maria, Nicky, and Angela. Ange, put the cheese tray on the table. Maria, get that crap out of the way. You hungry, Katherine? I got some nice peppers and a fresh loaf of bread all cut up. Anthony, where's your father?"

Any normal person would have been intimidated by the bombardment of questions and introductions, but Kate just smiled. "Thank you. It smells delicious."

If his mother smiled any harder she'd crack a tooth. "So, Anthony tells me your father's gonna give him a job. That's wonderful. My Ant's a hard worker. Smart too!"

His sister snorted and his mother, without breaking eye contact with Kate, smacked her in the back of the head. "Go find your father. You two, set the table. There's soda in the garage."

As his sisters left, he sat beside Kate and stuffed a slice of prosciutto in his mouth. Kate picked at a slice of bread and his mother continued to talk. "Do you have plans after graduation?"

"Just to work," Kate said.

"Good," his mother nodded. "You know who I talked to, Anthony? Your cousin Leo. He's workin' in the bar now." She shook her head. "Marlene's always talkin' about how smart he is, but he's not goin' to school next fall. He's gonna be workin'. I don't know what their thinkin'. Like my brother doesn't have the money to send him. He'll be makin' drinks for the rest of his life."

"You don't know that, Ma."

"We'll see." She gave him her all-knowing glare. "So Katherine, are you going to school in the fall?"

Her lips pursed. "Probably not this year. There are nine of us, so I have to save some money first."

"Nine?" His mom made the sign of the cross. "God bless your mother." His sisters returned and she immediately put them back to work.

"Nicky, stir the gravy. See if it's about done." Glancing back at Ant, she grumbled, "I told them to get those meatballs in by eleven, but no one listens to me. Eat some more, Katherine."

When the dining room table was set they moved to the

other room. His father waited at the head of the table in his white undershirt. "Pop, this is Kate."

His dad put down his glass of wine and stood. "Welcome. Did you eat? *Loretta,* where's the bread?" he shouted.

They sat at the side of the table across from his sister's empty chairs. His father filled Ant's glass with red wine and held the bottle up to Kate. "You?"

"Oh, no thank you."

His sisters, ceaselessly bickering, carried out steaming dishes of pasta braciole, homemade meatballs, and a boat of extra gravy. His mother followed with a tray of cutlets. Glancing at Kate, he smiled. "Told you there'd be lots of food."

"Oh my gawd, Ange, shut up," Maria argued as she jerked a chair out from the table, huffing as she sat. "I was only teasin'."

"Angela, stop arguing with your sister. We have company," his father barked, filling his plate and passing the pasta to Ant.

He passed Kate each bowl as they came around and she took a small sampling of everything. When she bit into the braciole she hummed pleasantly—almost sexually —and Ant's body took full notice.

"You like?" his mother asked, still not in her seat. "Here, have some more." She spooned another helping onto Kate's plate.

"It's delicious."

"Good. Eat up. You're too skinny. Anthony, do you have enough gravy?"

"I'm good, Ma."

His family talked all through dinner, not putting on airs for Kate and though he was nervous about bringing her to meet them, she never appeared overwhelmed or offended by anything they said. After dinner, his mother set the coffee pot on the table and his sisters took care of the dishes. His father reached to unbutton his pants, but Ant gave a shake of his head and he abstained.

"That's what you call a good meal. What did you think, Katherine?" his dad asked.

"It was amazing."

Ant smiled at her and whispered, "My mom's a good cook."

"She reminds me of my mother."

He could see that. "They'd probably get along."

After dinner they went out back and sat on the patio furniture. "This is my dad's favorite place," he told her, as he pulled his chair closer to hers. "He has an obsession with grass."

"I guess there wasn't a whole lot of that in the city."

"We had a small patch of lawn. He kept it *pristine*. It was his pride and joy. He'd sit out there on his lawn chair every Saturday—people watching."

Her smile tightened and she gave a soft laugh. "Well, there's plenty of land here. Do you miss the city?"

"Yes and no. It can get boring here, but it's much prettier." When she glanced at him from under her lashes, he touched her earring. "These are nice."

She self-consciously pulled at her earlobe. "They're my mom's. I borrowed them."

His stomach tightened with satisfaction. That meant she purposely put them on to see him. "I like them."

Since he'd already touched her he pushed his luck, catching her fingers in his and admiring her ring. "I like this too."

Her shoulders tightened but she didn't pull her hand from his. "I won't be in school tomorrow."

It was amazing how much that disappointed him. "How come?"

"I have a doctor's appointment."

"Will I see you tomorrow night? I have to meet your dad after school, but maybe after that?"

Her fingers pulled away. "Tomorrow might not be a great night. I have to see how tonight goes."

"Tonight?"

She folded her hands in her lap and eased back from the table. "I have to talk to my parents about some stuff. It might not go so well."

"Is everything okay?"

She nodded, but the tightness in her brow told a different story.

"You can talk to me, Kate." He wanted her to confide in him more than he wanted his next breath.

"Things are just complicated right now."

"Okay. But if you need an ear, I got two of them."

Sensing she wasn't ready to open up, he changed the subject to something lighter. "So…prom tickets go on sale tomorrow. You going?"

"No. I have to save money."

He frowned. He would have paid for her ticket. "I was thinking about it, but I need a date." When she looked at him, he arched a brow.

"Ant."

"You should go. It's our last hurrah."

Her smile turned sad. "I can't. I'd have to get a dress and the tickets are fifty dollars."

"Go with me. I'll buy the tickets." And his sisters had dresses. She could maybe borrow one of theirs.

She shook her head and it was difficult not to get discouraged. "Sorry. I can't. But you should go. I'm sure there are plenty of girls who would want to go with you."

"Nah. I have my heart set on one girl and if she's not going, neither am I."

She glanced at him. "Don't do that."

"Do what?" He eased closer, giving her his most cajoling smile. "Go to the prom with me, Katie."

"Ant, we aren't like that. We're just friends. Proms are for girlfriends and boyfriends."

His jaw twitched and he eased back. He was getting nowhere. Every time he thought he made some headway she was back to shutting him down. "All right. Then how about a movie? My treat."

She'd told his mother she had to work to pay for college and he knew how expensive that was. She was clearly taking the task seriously, being that she'd pass up prom, something he thought all girls were into.

"I can't."

Irritated, he sat back in his chair and stared at the house, trying to think of another way to get close to her. He was running out of ideas. "What if we went out with a group of friends?" He understood she needed time and he really wanted to give her that, but he also didn't want to extinguish any chance of showing her he was a decent guy.

"I'm not into hanging out with people lately."

"How about your brothers? We could go bowling. Luke and Finn would probably be into that." If they could manage that he might be able to get one of her brothers to act as a buffer and take a senior to prom, but that was pushing it. "Is Colin going to prom?"

She shook her head. "He's not even going to junior prom. I know what you're trying to do, Anthony, and it's sweet, but I'm not going."

Relenting, his shoulders drooped. He picked at the rubber of his shoe. "Is it me?"

"What? No."

"I don't understand. I want to take you out, Kate. We don't have to do anything. Why won't you give me a shot?"

"Because we're friends."

Inwardly, he growled. "You know I like you. Would it be so bad letting me take you out one time?" It wasn't like he couldn't be alone with her and resist the urge to kiss her, although it was getting tougher.

"It's not that."

"Then what? Is it because of your ex?" If he ever found out what guy hurt her he'd have a hard time resisting the urge to knock him out. "You can't stay single for the rest of your life because of one jerk."

"I just can't, okay?"

This wasn't going the way he hoped and he didn't mean to piss her off. He was just trying to understand her reluctance. "Do you want me to take you home?"

She reached for his wrist and checked his watch. "Yeah."

Disappointed, he stood. "I'll get my keys."

On the drive home she was quiet. He didn't understand why she wouldn't talk to him or at least give him a chance. Maybe he was wrong and the connection he felt was one-sided after all.

It was probably for the best she was missing school tomorrow. The more he saw her, the more he liked her, and she continued not to budge. He should probably put some distance between them until he got his emotions in check, because the last thing he wanted to do was make her feel cornered. Some asshole had already pressured her enough.

When they pulled up to her house the other cars were gone. He waited. This would be the time to kiss her, but there was no opening as she sat with her hands folded in her lap and her face was turned to the window. Plus the whole her not being interested thing. This sucked.

"Can I call you?" he asked.

She nodded so he gave her a piece of paper and a pen to write down her number. When she slid the paper back into his hand she said, "I might not be able to hang out for a while."

"Why?" Damn it. He should have never tried to pressure her about a date. He was screwing this all up and all he wanted to do was prove he could be patient, but he wanted her so much his head was a mess. Even if he couldn't have her, he wanted her friendship and if he didn't chill he was going to blow that too.

Rather than explain, she said, "Call me tomorrow night and I'll let you know how things are."

Frowning, he nodded. "Okay."

He watched her slowly take the steps up to the porch. When she got to the door, she turned back and raised her hand in a wave. Something was off and he didn't have a clue what it could be, which meant it was most likely him. He'd thought they had a nice day. She liked his family. They laughed all throughout dinner. She wore earrings. He was at a loss.

Pursing his lips, he backed out of her drive and decided he'd call her tomorrow night after he *hopefully* landed a job with her father. McCulloughs were definitely a tough bunch to impress.

CHAPTER 8

Kate entered the house and watched Ant's car pull away. She'd never wanted to kiss someone as desperately as she wanted to kiss him today. If they hadn't left when they had, she might have agreed to let him take her to prom. She could have borrowed a dress, but that would have complicated everything even more. It took everything she had not to give in, but she liked him enough to know he didn't deserve being caught up in a problematic situation.

"Katie," her mother's voice softly called.

She turned and sighed. Time to face the music. "Is Daddy here?"

Her mother nodded and untied her apron. "He's in the den. Are you ready?"

No. But there was no preparing for this. "Should we talk in the kitchen?"

"That's probably best. I made some rice pudding. Why don't you have a bowl and I'll go get your father."

"Where's everyone else?"

"I sent them to Rosemarie's for a while."

"Do the aunts know?"

Her mother's smile was apologetic. "I told them, but only so they could tell your uncles. Your father will need some sense talked into him and I'm hoping they might be some help."

Kate went to the kitchen, but didn't have the stomach for pudding. She sat at the table and her entire body trembled as her stomach churned. She tried to imagine how her father looked at her, the way his eyes lit when he saw her. She locked those images away in her mind for safekeeping. Her greatest fear was that he'd never look at her like that again.

The moment her parents entered the kitchen, her father looked suspicious. He sat across from her and smirked. "It's never good to come to a table set for talking. Maureen, how about some coffee, love?" He yawned.

Her mother went about setting up the coffee pot and her father stared at her expectantly, but she couldn't find her voice.

"Is this about you wanting that job? We already have a secretary, Katie girl. You'd be better off finding something fulltime."

She'd wanted the job because all of her brothers were expected to work at the yard and it just seemed fair to do the same. But maybe he was right and she should find something fulltime. She supposed she could waitress.

Her mother took a seat at her side and patted her arm. "Katherine has something to tell you, Frank."

He raised a brow. "Oh? Did you get a letter from a college?"

God, she was such a letdown. She'd gotten a letter a week ago, telling her she was accepted at the community college, but she made sure to intercept the mail, knowing her father would rather see her go off to school. School wasn't an option at the moment. She needed to work.

"Go ahead, dear," her mother coaxed softly.

She drew in a deep breath. "I'm not going to go to school this year, Dad."

His lips twisted. "Because you want to live alone? Listen to me, lass. You go to the community college, get your Associates, and in two years you can go off and live wherever you want while you finish your degree. You do that, and I'll give you a part time position at the office."

Her throat tightened. She couldn't meet his gaze. "I can't."

"Katherine, you're going to want more than I can pay you when you're in your twenties. The good jobs go to kids with an education. I told you I'll help you with the loan papers and pay whatever we can. I don't know why you're fighting me on this." He looked at her mother. "Since when are you silent?"

Her mother drew in a breath and gave her father a

stern look. Without raising her voice, she said, "Katherine won't be going to college this year, Frank."

He rolled his eyes, looking away from the table in clear irritation. "This is ridiculous. She can work and go to school. Give me one reason—"

"I'm pregnant."

Silence.

Every hair on her body stood on end as her vision blurred. "So I won't be going back to school this year or the next. I know what I did and I know how disappointed you must be and I'm sorry, but what I need is a job."

She'd memorized every nick and divot on the table, but still looked for more as she lowered her head. She couldn't seem to lift her face to meet his eyes. "I'm sorry," she whispered, as a tear fell to the worn surface.

"I'll get the coffee." Her mother rose and her abandonment resonated, tension pressing hard into Kate's shoulders.

Swallowing the thick lump in her throat, she forced herself to look at her father. Nothing prepared her for the devastation she found in his eyes. More tears gathered at her lashes and fell unchecked down her face. "I'm so sorry, Daddy."

His mouth was flat, his eyes the darkest shade of blue she'd ever seen. The only movement came with the rise of his shoulders under each heavy breath and the slight twitch in his jaw.

Her mother placed a cup of coffee on the table and he

broke eye contact. She returned to Kate's side and they silently waited for him to respond.

Without touching the mug, he rose and walked out the kitchen door letting it slam behind him. As Kate stared at his back she fell to pieces, sobbing quietly as her mother pulled her into her arms. "Give him a minute, love."

"He hates me."

"No, dear. Your father loves you. Nothing will ever change that." She kissed her head and brushed her hair away from her wet cheeks. "Men need time to process. Right now he's just thinking of what this means. You have to understand. You were his first baby, his little girl. As a father of seven he knows quite well where babies come from and right now he's protecting you the best he knows how by carrying himself outside until he calms down."

She wiped her eyes, but her tears continued to flow. They waited a long time for him to come in off the porch. Her mother had two cups of coffee and forced Kate to eat some pudding, but she wasn't hungry and could only stomach a few bites.

They kept their voices low as they waited. "I was thinking we could clean up Sheilagh's cradle for you. That would fit nice in your room."

She couldn't think of things like that when she didn't feel welcome in her own home.

"And I still have a changing table in the attic. It's fairly new, being that Luke and Finnegan destroyed theirs. Pray for a girl, dear. Boys break everything. So destructive."

The screen opened and she looked up at her father

expectantly. His face was devoid of emotion. "You knew about this, Maureen?"

Her mother stammered. "I only just found out."

He nodded and glanced at Kate. Though his eyes were nothing more than sad, his detached gaze crushed her. "You can start work as soon as you finish the school year." He hesitated and shook his head then walked out of the kitchen. His steps echoed through the silent house as he took the stairs.

When a door slammed on the second floor, she flinched. Her mother sighed and said, "Well, you have the job you wanted. That's a plus."

CHAPTER 9

*A*nt glanced at his resume checking it over one last time as he waited in the trailer for Mr. McCullough. The secretary had called to let him know he was there almost twenty minutes ago. He'd thought they had an appointment, but supposed the man forgot and was busy with other things. He'd offered to come back at another time, but the secretary told him Mr. McCullough insisted he stay put. So he waited.

As he watched the clock another fifteen minutes passed. He wanted the job, but this was bordering on plain rude. He should have made an appointment and come back later. The phone on the secretary's desk rang.

"McCullough Lumber. Okay, Frank." She hung up the phone. "He's waiting for you out front."

Finally. Ant stood and left the trailer, coming up short when he saw Mr. McCullough leaning up against a work truck taking his full measure. Jesus, the guy was intimidating. The mere breadth of his shoulders was two times thicker than the guys on the field, fully suited for a game.

He held out his resume. "Sorry if I got the time wrong."

Kate's father's eyes narrowed and he took the resume without a word, giving it only a partial glance before folding it in half and stuffing it in the pocket of his flannel. He eased his bulk off the truck and gruffly ordered, "Get in."

Ant didn't know where they were going, but if he was planning on showing him around the yard that was good sign. Hopefully it meant he had the job. He climbed into the passenger side of the truck and stilled when he saw the ax leaning up against the dashboard.

He was being ridiculous. Shutting the door, he waited for Mr. McCullough. The man slid behind the wheel and gripped the stick shift. His arms were corded with thick muscle and covered in dark hair. Nicks and divots of white scars spattered across his tanned skin. This was a guy who had obviously taken a few lumps in his day.

He didn't drive them where Kate had taken him. They drove so deep in the woods Ant's sense of direction got turned around. Thank God Mr. McCullough was familiar with the land, because Ant wouldn't have been able to find his way back if he tried.

The truck pulled over on a mud road outside of a small shack. Mr. McCullough grabbed the ax and said, "Get out."

Unsure if this was his natural disposition or if he simply didn't like him, Ant set his mind to proving himself. He followed Mr. McCullough to a long tree that appeared to have fallen that winter. The gnarled roots were dry and stood a good ten feet above the ground.

A stump from a different tree was next to the fallen trunk and Ant paused as Mr. McCullough swung the ax with one hand and buried it in the center of the stump. "You see that ax, son?"

Ant nodded. "Yes, sir."

"It's mine. You touch it and I'll break your legs." He walked back to the truck and Ant stood staring at the glint of sunlight catching the blade wedged into the stump.

Okay, he definitely wasn't imagining things. Kate's dad did not like him. Leaves crunched as the man approached and chains jangled as he tossed them by Ant's feet. He glanced at Mr. McCullough and took a jerky step back as he yanked the cord of a chainsaw and brought it to life. This was definitely not the meeting he'd anticipated.

The woods echoed with the churning buzz of the saw as Mr. McCullough simply stared at him and kept the motor going. Ant waited for the echo of banjos from *Deliverance* in the distance. Swallowing, he glanced at the little shack.

The saw silenced. "You see that tree?"

Ant looked back at the tree and nodded.

"Also mine." Mr. McCullough carried the saw to the stump and placed it on the ground. Extracting the ax with one hand, he examined the blade. "This whole mountain's mine and that includes everything—and everyone—on it. You understand?"

"Yes, sir." If this was a question of his honorability, he was sure his previous employer would give him a decent recommendation.

"I don't take kindly to other men trespassing on my property."

Oh fuck. This was about the falls. "Sir, it was only a couple times."

His eyes snapped to him and narrowed. Somehow that had been the wrong thing to say.

"It won't happen again." Damn. This guy really didn't like trespassers. "I hope this doesn't interfere with my application. I'm a hard worker and I hardly ever call out."

"You're damn right it won't happen again. That's my daughter. My *first* daughter. I ought to kill you, but that won't solve the mess you two got yourselves in."

Ant frowned, completely lost. "Is this about the falls?"

Mr. McCullough's head turned, the weathered skin at his neck dark with stubble. "*My* falls?" He took a menacing step toward him and drew an audible breath in through his nose, the ax gripped tight in his hand. "Let me make this clear to you, boy. This is my mountain. These are my trees. Those are my falls. And Katherine is *my* daughter."

He was going to die.

Swallowing, he took a pace back. "With all due respect, sir, she's an adult."

Big mistake.

His eyes contracted into little slits and Ant was certain he wasn't getting the job now. He was sort of okay with that, being that Kate's dad was turning out to be a psychopath with lots of sharp toys.

"You think you have it all figured out, don't you, son?" His clipped laugh was menacing. "I'll tell you what. You have all the answers? Find your own way back." He turned and grabbed the chainsaw, carrying it with the ax back to the truck. Leaving the chains, he climbed into the truck and the engine roared.

"You have to be joking?" Ant mumbled under his breath, sure this was some sort of test. But then the truck peeled out on the muddy road and he was standing there next to some creepy, fucked up, serial killer shack and a downed tree.

He smacked his arm as a mosquito bit him. "What the fuck just happened?"

He scanned the woods and listened for any sounds of traffic. All he heard were animals scurrying across the brambles and wind blowing through the trees. He decided to follow the mud tracks back.

After about thirty minutes of walking, he was certain he was lost. Dirt roads crisscrossed every few hundred yards and some pretty strange looking bugs had bitten him. He caught sight of a few chipmunks and a deer, which was exciting at first, but as the sun began to set he started thinking about other animals, bigger animals, and walked a little faster.

His sneakers were not cut out for this sort of terrain. He'd intended to invest in boots if he got the job, but that wasn't happening now. The longer he walked the more everything started looking the same. Nasty moths that looked like spiders with wings clung to trees and if he didn't find people again soon, he was going to die up on this mountain.

His mouth was dry. His back was sweating. And he had blisters on his feet. As he hiked, his jaw clenched tighter and tighter. Kate's dad was a fucking nutcase. Why the hell would he leave someone in the middle of woods unless he hoped they'd die? Ant was a little worried he might not live long enough to tell the man exactly where he could shove his ax and crappy job. At this rate, he never wanted to set foot in the woods again.

When dusk turned to darkness, he was certain he'd be sleeping in the wilderness. His legs were tired and he couldn't see shit, tripping every few steps over roots and rocks. He was starving and getting nowhere, so he paused to take a rest by a tree.

"Hello?" he yelled then smacked his shoulder as something else bit him.

"Can anyone hear me?" he screamed, his voice reverberating in a drifting echo as it passed through the endless trees. "I've been left in the woods by a fucking lunatic!" The echo gave no inclination of where he was.

"I'm in the fucking Blair Witch Project," he growled, moving on as something with big ass wings buzzed past his ear. *Jesus!*

Why the hell hadn't he been a boy scout? He tried to find some stars in the sky, but when he could see past the canopy of trees he had no freaking idea how the Big

Dipper was going to help him. If that was the Big Dipper anyway.

He was going to die there. A bear was going to get him or a million mosquitos. *"Fuck!"* he roared sending little things scurrying through the brush.

He itched under his clothes, certain bugs were crawling on him. He was back on a muddy path, but not one he recognized. Or maybe he did. Everything was black and looked fucking identical. He should have stayed at the little shack.

Pressing the button on his watch offered the only light he had, not that it helped. Eight-thirty. He'd been walking for almost four hours. Turning in a circle, he lost his sense of direction again, unsure if he was back-tracking or moving away from the direction he'd just come. Squinting, he saw something in the distance, a subtle light. Maybe it was just the reflection of the moon on the trees, but he followed it, desperate to get out of the darkness.

His feet crunched over sticks and leaves, snapping twigs and slipping over rocks, but the more he walked the more he could make out the distant light. It was coming from something, maybe the freeway. The woods thinned and stumps filled a long spread of land, making it easier to see. His breath caught as he made out the silhouette of a house in the distance.

"Thank God." Jogging, he ran toward the house and panted. "I just need a phone. I'll call Pop for a ride and—" He scowled, his steps stumbling to a halt when he recognized the house. "Son of a bitch." Mr. McCullough's truck was parked right out front.

Seething, he stumbled down the hill, lurching, as his legs were practically numb from hiking. His brain played on a steady ramble of insults. *Crazy motherfucker. How about I stick that ax right up your ass? I probably have twenty spider bites and at least ten ticks on me. I should drag your ass back to that shed and lock you inside with a wasp hive. Like to see how tough you are then, you psycho son of a bitch.*

His feet stumbled as he neared the house. His dry mouth was no match for the roar building in his chest. *"McCullough!"* he yelled, his voice echoing off the surrounding trees.

He didn't care that the guy was Kate's dad. It didn't matter that he had more than twenty years on him. He gave not *one* shit that he was on his precious property. He could have died in those woods! And he was not going to let it slide.

"Get out here, you crazy fuck!"

As he crossed the field the front door opened and Mr. McCullough's burly form stepped onto the porch, arms crossed. Ant glared at him, his eyes burning from sweat and the side of his face swollen from some bite he'd gotten in the last mile or so.

"You left me there to die!" he shouted, crossing the driveway.

Another door opened and Mrs. McCullough came out and gasped. "Oh dear." Her fingers wrung a dishtowel and she looked at her husband. "Frank, what have you done?"

He had nothing against Kate's mom, but he was not going to take this lying down. "Do you have a problem with me? Did I do something to you? What the hell kind of guy leaves another man in the woods like that?"

One by one Kate's siblings came out of the kitchen and gaped at him as he stood on the driveway shouting at their father. When Kate came out she gasped. *"Anthony?"*

He glared at her, unsure if *any* girl was worth this sort of insanity.

Her fingers covered her mouth as she glanced at her father and back to him. "What happened to you?"

"Your father drove me into the woods, showed me his chainsaw, then left me in the middle of fucking nowhere!"

Her wide eyes turned to her father, who made no attempt to deny a single accusation. She visibly shook as she glared at him. A shrill voice came out of her as her hands balled into fists. "What the hell is the matter with you? Why would you do that?"

Without giving him a chance to answer, she rushed down the porch steps and set her attention on him. "You've been eaten alive by mosquitos." When she touched his cheek he jerked back, not trusting a single one of them.

"Colin, go get the first aid kit. The rest of you back to bed," her mother ordered, pushing the kids back inside.

Ant continued to glare at her father as Kate looked up at him. "I don't know why he'd do this. I'm sorry."

Mrs. McCullough waited for Kate's brother to return and when he did, she hustled off the porch and came to examine his face, tsking. "You come with me, Anthony. I'll clean up these bites. I think I have some Benadryl to help with the itching."

"I'm not going up there," he growled, eyes hard on Kate's dad.

Mrs. McCullough looked over her shoulder and scoffed. "You should be ashamed of yourself, Frank. He's done nothing you didn't do when you were his age."

Kate shook her head, looking back at her dad, clearly upset. "I don't understand why you would—" Her words cut off, as something seemed to occur to her and her back stiffened. "Daddy!" she snapped sharply. "It's not *him.*"

Something happened in that moment. Mrs. McCullough looked at her daughter with wide eyes and Mr. McCullough's face paled, all signs of menace leaving his scowl at once as he croaked, "What?"

Kate glared at him, her hands forming tight fists at her side again. "Even if it was, you had no right to do this! He could have died in those woods! Are you insane?" she practically screeched.

"I thought—"

She turned away from him, her eyes shimmering. "Come inside and let me clean you up."

He wasn't sure what was happening, but Mr. McCullough lowered his head, seeming to deflate before their eyes, and walked to his truck. His wife and daughter scowled at him as he turned on the engine and drove away.

The next several minutes were passed in a flurry of

motion. Kate cleaned the scratches on his arms and doctored the bug bites at his neck and face while her mother practically force fed him ham and pudding, while taking long pulls from a bottle of whiskey she found under the sink.

They were very apologetic and he was happy to finally be sitting down. Once his rage cooled and his thirst was quenched, Mrs. McCullough left them alone in the kitchen.

"I'm so sorry, Anthony. I had no idea he'd do anything like that. *Especially* to you."

He looked at her, scrutinizing her sincerity and unsure if he could survive this family. Her hands continued to touch his arms, which helped calm him down, but didn't take away his frustration. "Your dad's a fucking maniac, Kate."

"He's really not. Usually my mum's the crazy one. You just caught him on a bad day."

He scoffed. "A bad day? Kate, he just left me there."

"I know, but he would have said something eventually and I would have come to find you."

He shook his head. They were all crazy. And the man made it pretty clear he didn't want him dating his daughter. The longer he stayed around them the more nuts it seemed to even want to get close to her. He was catching their insanity. And for what? "I have to go."

Her brow puckered. "Please don't let this ruin our friendship. I'll talk to my dad and get him to apologize."

"I don't want his freaking apology." Didn't they realize

how foreign those woods were to people who didn't grow up there?

"Then tell me how to make it right," she pleaded, gripping his arm.

He glanced around the kitchen, searching for an answer. This was just too much. He liked Kate—liked her a lot—but she wanted a friend and he cared about her in a different way. Her father was a step away from being a backwoods murderer and he didn't know how much more he could survive.

He'd said he could take it slow and was willing to put in his time, but this was crazy. She wasn't interested in him and her father tried to kill him. Okay, maybe he was being dramatic. He'd made it out of the woods with only a few bites, blisters, and scratches, but none of that needed to happen.

Looking into her green-blue eyes, he shook his head, wishing he could offer more. "This isn't working for me, Kate. I'm sorry."

Her mouth pursed as her chin trembled. He hated hurting her. Brow pinched, she nodded. "I understand."

He looked away. Still, he got nothing from her, not even a push for him to hold out a little longer. He was tired of being hurt when she'd been nothing but clear about her feelings. It was his own damn fault for forcing something that clearly wasn't there. She wasn't interested and he had to move on, get away from them for a while, for his own good and hers. "Can you give me a ride to my car?"

She stood and collected her keys from the counter without a word. She was silent as they drove to the trailer and, as she pulled her car next to his, she still didn't speak.

"I guess I'll see you around," he mumbled, opening the door and digging out his keys.

"Anthony, wait." She got out of the car and rounded the front, stopping just in front of the headlights.

He paused, only a foot away from her and waited. He had nothing left to say.

She wrung her hands and whispered, "I don't want to lose you."

Glancing at the woods, he rolled his eyes. "What do you want from me, Kate? A friend? I tried taking it slow, but this isn't a pace thing, it's a never thing. All you want is a friend and you know damn well I like you more than that. Your dad threatened me with a fucking chainsaw—"

"I'm sorry!"

"Well, maybe sorry doesn't fix it! Jesus! I could still be out there. I didn't know where I was. It's black as shit in the woods at night and I'm pretty sure I heard a bear. I'm not from here. Where I come from, people don't do shit like that—"

His words stifled as she took a step forward and pressed her lips to his. Everything in him went still. His hands lifted, catching her hips and holding her there as if she were a fantasy that might fade into thin air.

"I don't want to lose you," she whispered against his lips, slowly pulling back and blinking up at him.

His heart raced as he tried to understand what this

meant. Was this a pity kiss, some last ditch attempt at saving their friendship? He couldn't handle any more games. "What was that? Why did you kiss me?"

Her face lowered and he caught her chin, needing to see her eyes. "Tell me, Kate."

Her lips parted, those beautiful blue eyes shifting to green in the light casting from her car as she blinked quickly. "I wanted to kiss you for a long time, but I knew it was wrong."

How could she say that? What was wrong with him? "Why?"

She shook her head and sniffled, the porcelain skin around her nose flushing as her eyes shimmered with unshed tears. "Because, no matter how I feel, I can't go out with you, Anthony."

"But you feel *something*? Something more than friendship?"

Her lips twisted as her lashes spiked. Why was this so hard for her? "I feel more for you than I've ever felt for any guy."

"Then why can't we be together? What's the problem? Is it your dad?"

"No. It's me." Her shoulders shook on a choppy breath.

He was done with guessing. "Tell me the truth, Kate. What's going on?"

Her face lowered and she croaked, "Anthony, I'm having a baby."

His face went numb and his hands fell away. "What?"

She took a step back, collecting herself, that impenetrable mask she hid behind snuffing out her tears. "I'm pregnant. That's why I can't go to prom and why I'm not going to college in the fall and why I can't be your girlfriend."

His brain awkwardly pieced together her words, but they still only made clumsy sense. Pregnant? How? Since when? This couldn't be right.

Shaking his head, he frowned. "Who's the father?" *Holy shit.* Was the father the guy that took her virginity after barely asking?

Her eyes pinched shut as if answering caused her physical pain. "Nick Porter, but you can't tell *anyone.* I'm only telling you, because you're the only friend I have right now and I trust you."

"No one else knows it's his?"

"Just my brother Colin, but he won't tell. He gave me his word."

He searched his mind for a face that matched the name. He knew of three Nicks. One didn't have a chance in hell at getting with a girl like Kate. The other didn't seem her type. The third, well, he didn't seem her type either, but he had a reputation for sleeping around. "Nick the lacrosse player?"

Her chin trembled as worry flashed in her eyes. "Are you friends with him?"

Hardly, the guy was a scumbag, the sort that would suck his own dick if he could reach it. He never stopped bragging and the few times Ant had been in his presence he hadn't stuck around. "No, but I know who he is. Does he know about the baby?"

She nodded. "Yes, but he isn't going to be involved. He wanted me to have an abortion and I didn't want that."

His molars locked as he imagined her having that argument with an asshole like Porter alone. "Jesus, Kate. Is that why you went to the doctor's today?"

She nodded and another thought occurred to him.

"Your dad thought *I* was the father." In a strange way this redeemed the man a small degree. He blew out a long breath and gripped the back of his neck. "A baby." It wasn't like she was the first to be in this position. Plenty of girls were pregnant in his old high school. Accidents happened. "Are *you* okay?"

She winced. "Don't do that. Don't worry about me after the night you've—"

He rolled his eyes and gripped her shoulders. "Are. You. Okay?"

She shrugged, her posture stiff, but her gaze telling him how much her strength cost her. "I'm handling it the best I can."

"Fuck, Katie, I had no idea."

She seemed ready to shatter, but maybe others couldn't see what he saw when he looked into her eyes. He'd come to memorize every detail of each of her expressions, but now she was showing him her vulnerability and it gutted him.

"That's why you were sick the other day, isn't it?"

"That was the first time that happened. I wanted to tell

you, but it's still new and I didn't want you to look at me differently. I'm sorry I lied."

"You didn't lie." Not really. She just left out a serious detail. "Pregnant," he repeated, still processing.

She made a sound that was almost a laugh, but too full of pain to be any sign of joy. "Now do you see why I can't go out with you?"

He glanced at her, waiting for something to click, some signal that she was different from the girl she was a few minutes ago. But she was just Kate. "I don't know. I don't know how I feel right now."

She licked her lips, her eyes downcast, and whispered, "Well, at least you know the truth."

He now understood why she was so resistant, but he didn't necessarily know if that changed his feelings. Stepping close to her, he laced his fingers in hers. "Come here."

She took a small step forward and he'd thought to kiss her, but then he simply pulled her into a hug and held her. "I'm still your friend, Katie. Nothing could change that." He shut his eyes, letting her warmth seep through his clothes as he tightened his hold. "I'm glad you confided in me."

As her arms pulled around him, holding him close, he tried to remember ever feeling anything that felt that good, that right, but nothing compared. He pressed his face into her shoulder and breathed through her thick hair, pulling her scent deep and committing it to memory. He didn't know what it was about her, but he couldn't get enough.

So she was pregnant. Definitely a complication, but what if he never felt this connection with another girl again? She was funny and sweet and bold yet fragile. Despite everything he just found out, his greatest fear was that Nick Porter might come to his senses and take her away from him.

"Are you sure Nick doesn't want to be involved?"

"He's known for three weeks and hasn't contacted me. He offered to take me to a clinic, but that was it. Plus, he's dating my ex-best friend and cheating on her with some freshman. I'm relieved he's out of the picture."

But that meant she'd have to do everything on her own. "What about adoption?"

"The baby's mine, Ant."

"You can still make him pay child support."

"I don't want anything from him."

He tried to imagine her a year from now, tried to picture if she'd have a boy or a girl. He'd be in college, more than halfway through his freshman year. His mind broke his future into increments. Four years wasn't that long. He still hadn't signed the papers for housing, though he had the scholarship. Damn. Was she worth sticking around and commuting?

Maybe.

They had to start being honest with each other. He pulled back and looked at her, his hands gently cupping the sides of her face. "Katie, when I said I liked you, I meant it. I don't know if that's changed."

"Maybe you should sleep on it."

Probably, but he didn't want to. He wanted her. His head was in a spin bin. "Will you be in school tomorrow?"

"Yes."

Of course she would. Everything was exactly the same, except there was a baby inside of her. "You jumped off the rope swings. Should you have done that?"

"Probably not, but my doctor said I can do everything I usually do as far as physical activity."

God, this was a lot to digest. Strange things kept occurring to him. The way she ate. The fact that she never had caffeinated beverages. How she said she didn't drink alcohol anymore. The moment he found her crying in the car. The constant trips to the bathroom. Without thinking, his hand went to her stomach and gently pressed.

She sucked in a breath and looked up at him, her eyes unguarded for a change. She was growing a person in there. Searching her trusting gaze, he couldn't see how that should take away from all the other awesome parts of her.

Tilting his head, he brushed his lips to hers and his body shivered. Yes, he still wanted her. His mouth teased hers softly, coaxing her into the kiss and gradually she rose on her toes and slid her arms over his shoulders. All his tension fled as her tongue gently brushed his.

His hands slid from her stomach, around her back and pulled her flush against his front. He'd waited so long to taste her, had countless fantasies about kissing her and touching her.

Her fingers teased the ends of his hair and he breathed

deep, her scent filling him like a drug. Sliding his palms down her spine, he lowered them to her plump little ass and squeezed, drawing the softest moan from her mouth.

He deepened the kiss. His hands massaged her curves, dragging over her clothes, and soon his fingers were buried in her thick hair.

His body hardened and ached with need. Trying to slow down, he thought of her dad and his big fucking ax, but even that didn't impede his desire. She felt too good, tasted too sweet, and kissed better than anyone he'd ever kissed.

Breathing raggedly, he whispered, "We should slow down."

"What's the point?"

He dropped his hands and forced himself to take a step back. "The point is I care about you and I don't want to rush you."

"I care about you too, Anthony."

To hear her say those words was like breathing after a lifetime under water. He took another step back and adjusted his clothes, which seemed too tight against his frame. He needed to keep his head. "We aren't going to rush things, Kate."

"I get it." A dejected look stole over her eyes.

"Get what? I'm just saying we should take it slow."

She glanced at his car. "I should probably get back, and your parents are probably waiting for you."

"Why do I get the feeling you're blowing me off?"

"Anthony…" She shook her head, no longer looking at

him. "I know how you feel, because I feel it too. But sooner or later, you're going to realize there isn't a simple solution to this. And when you do, you'll go away and it'll be over. I can accept that, because you have a lot of opportunities coming up that I don't. I tried to pretend I didn't feel anything for you, but I feel so much. The lies are starting to hurt."

"What lies?"

Her lashes lifted and he recognized stark desperation in her gaze. "Once this baby's born I don't know when someone else will ask me out on a date again. I don't know if I'll ever like someone as much as I like you, because I never wanted to be with someone the way I want to be with you. Even when you're not there, you're on my mind, making me smile. Maybe... we could just make the best of the summer and at least take the memory with us when we go our separate ways. I understand our paths are going in different directions. It's all I've thought about since I met you."

He wanted to tell her that wouldn't happen, but he couldn't. She was right. Eventually, she'd have a baby, *a child*. She'd be a mother, doing motherly things while he was blowing off steam at frat parties and keggers. Perhaps the summer was all they had together. It could either be great or a dragged out period of avoidance while they waited for their lives to begin.

There was no doubt it would be challenging keeping away from her. He wanted whatever he could get while he was still close by. Because the truth was, he thought about her every second of the day since meeting her and he honestly didn't know how to stop. He didn't know what would happen in the fall when they went their separate ways, because his imagination could only take him so far.

He wanted more than a few weeks, but the reality was, that was the most either of them could offer. Pulling her to him again, he looked into her eyes. "Then let's make it the best summer either of us have ever had."

"Really?" Her smile was the prettiest thing he'd seen since moving to Center County.

God, how could he deny either of them? "Really."

CHAPTER 10

Kate stepped through the front door and quietly hung her keys on the wall.

"Katie girl, is that you?" Her jaw tightened as she heard her father's voice.

She was surprised he'd waited up. Stepping into the dim kitchen, she paused at the door. "I have nothing to say to you."

His blue eyes were tight with regret. "I waited for you," he rasped. "That's what a father does. He waits even when he knows his children are old enough to take care of themselves, and he worries, no matter how much he knows they can handle things on their own."

Blinking, she glanced at the wall. "What you did to Anthony was wrong on so many levels, Dad. I don't know what to say."

"I was wrong. I made a mistake. But you'll understand my reaction soon enough." He shook his head, his gaze falling to the table as he spread his fingers wide and held out his hands. "I still remember holding you in my palms like it was yesterday. You were my first. The first baby I ever got to truly hold. I wanted everything for you." His voice cracked. "I wanted to give you every possible opportunity a man can give his daughter."

A tear dripped down her cheek. "I made a mistake, Daddy. But it was my accident. I can't go through the rest of my life punishing myself for it or carrying around anger toward some guy when neither of us meant for this to happen. I just want to move on the best I can."

When he looked at her again, his blue gaze trembled, the whites of his eyes shot with pink. "Are you sure this is what you want? I know… the church has strong opinions about such things, but…you're my little girl and I'll support you no matter what you choose. I'll always be there for you, baby."

Her chest quavered as she lost the battle against her tears and choked on a sob. "Thank you, Daddy." She bit down on her lip as her throat clogged with emotion. "I know what my choices are and I've already made up my mind. I want to keep the baby."

His chair scraped along the wooden floor as he rose. She wiped her eyes, but there was no containing her tears. When he pulled her into his strong arms, arms that had always protected her, she clung to him. His strength was beyond measure. Flashes from her childhood leapt to mind as he hugged her tight. Climbing onto his shoulders as she and her brothers played king of the mountain.

Having him guide her hands the first time she drew back a bow. His clumsy fingers holding the daintiest teacup as he sat in her grandmother's pearls and sipped the best air.

"I love you, Daddy."

"I love you too, Katie girl." He cleared his throat and kissed her hair, releasing her. His broad back filled her view, but she saw him wipe his tears on the heel of his palm. "I need a drink."

She laughed. "Me too."

He mockingly glanced over his shoulder.

She sat at the table, feeling as if she could finally breathe for the first time in weeks. Her father found her mother's whiskey stash under the sink and grabbed two mugs and a gallon of milk. Sitting across from her, he filled one mug, almost to the brim with whiskey and the other with cold milk. He slid her the milk and she clinked her mug to his. They both hummed at the same time and laughed.

"So…" he said, his thumb rolling over the handle of his mug. "If Ant's not the father…"

"Dad."

"You know I expect a name."

"Why, so you can drive him to the woods and threaten him with power tools?"

"There are other reasons."

"You want to pressure me to marry him? That isn't happening. It's the nineties."

"This guy's absence tells me more about his character than his presence ever could, Katherine. That being said, even if he wanted to marry you, I'd say no. That could change, but right now I'm bettin' he's not the sort of man I'd respect."

He was right about that. "You know, I never thought I'd be in this position," she confessed. "I wasn't prepared to make such big decisions. It's a little unfair to the men in these situations, when they want to choose something else and the girl's the one who has the final say. I won't force him to be a part of this."

"Women take the brunt of the responsibility, honey. I love all of you kids, but there hasn't been a day yet that I've outshined your mother. She does everything for you kids and she's had her fair share of loss too. Loss has a way of keeping with females when we men somehow bury the hurt until it can't touch us anymore."

Her parents had been together since they were young and she supposed they had their own story to tell. She had no doubt they both dealt with heartache and she was grateful her father at least assured her that pain faded in time. She needed to know that.

"I don't think I'm strong enough to handle what giving the baby up might do to me—even if it went to a good home. It's part of me."

"Then I think you're making the right choice, but it *is* your choice and I'll support you no matter what."

"The guy...he wanted me to..."

Her father's hand slid across the table and gripped hers. "He's not here."

She smiled at him and squeezed his calloused fingers.

No matter how hard she squeezed, she knew he could take it. "Will you teach the baby things I can't?"

"Like what? You're as fierce as any one of your brothers."

She shrugged. "I don't know. If it's a boy, teach him how to pitch overhand. And if it's a girl, be her hero in any way she needs."

His smile turned soft. "We'll leave the lessons on swearing and farting up to your mother." They both laughed.

They talked until sometime after midnight, discussing everything, but he never brought up the baby's father again. It was sometime in the wee hours of the night, as she lay in bed, playing back all the things he'd said, that she decided the baby's name. If she had a girl, she'd call her Frances. And if it was a boy, she'd spell it with an *I*, but he'd go by Frank for short.

EVERYTHING SEEMED to come together in the following weeks. Though Kate's social life had taken a pathetic turn, she didn't mind spending her evenings yelling at the contestants of *Wheel of Fortune* with her parents or helping her mother in the kitchen. Ant often came by and, once her father apologized, he seemed to make amends with the other man in her life.

She told Finn, Luke, and Braydon about the baby first, but soon enough Kelly and Sheilagh found out. While the younger ones didn't seem overly concerned that the baby was without a father, Finn and Luke were quite bothered by the fact. Colin kept his word and avoided rooms whenever the conversation came up, but as the weeks passed and no name was delivered, they all seemed to drop it.

The aunts were over the moon at the idea of a new baby to love, which removed the fear of any shame Kate thought might come. At her second doctor's appointment she noticed three other girls in the waiting room that looked about her age. She no longer understood why she was so worried she'd feel like a pariah when young moms were popping up all over the place.

They were in the grocery store, at the library, and even at church. She suspected there were even a few she couldn't tell because they weren't showing yet. And though times had changed, she was no younger than her mother was when she had her.

She'd worried about church, because her family was the loud, obnoxious family at every mass, but even that turned out okay. She went to confession, said a few rosaries, and the following Sunday during mass the priest made the sign of the cross over her belly during communion.

It all seemed too easy. And sometimes, when her family encircled her and their love and support surrounded her without question, her emotions gained on her and she had to work to keep herself together. She was truly blessed to have such an incredible family and though they were all a little insane, she wouldn't trade them for the world.

The only problem she really had, as graduation approached, was finding pants that didn't cut into her stomach and finding quiet places she and Anthony could make out without being interrupted by her younger siblings. She'd heard women talk about all sorts of cravings, pickles with peanut butter, smoked herring, mustard on everything. But the only thing she truly craved was Anthony.

She craved his kisses, his glances, his laughter, his smiles, and most of all, his hugs. How she ever thought to deny her feelings for him made her just as crazy as every other McCullough. Sometimes, when they were together, she missed him, because even having him right there wasn't always enough. She was addicted to him and couldn't get enough regardless of how frequently he stopped by, which was almost every day.

He was extremely affectionate, always holding her hand and touching her hair, but he never let things go farther than a few kisses. And whenever things seemed like they might move to the next stage, he pulled back. She didn't know if it was the baby that made him uncomfortable or the fact that her father had gone hillbilly on his ass. But it was starting to piss her off that he wouldn't touch her boobs.

One night, as they fooled around in his car, she pulled his hand to her bra. Ant immediately pulled away and she huffed. "What's the matter, Anthony? They're not going to shoot milk at you."

"I know that." He faced the wheel, his cheeks flushed. "Jesus, Katie, your parents could come out at any second."

"Anthony, I think they know I've had sex."

He glared at her, unimpressed. "That's not funny."

"Ant, we've been dating for over a month. I think it's okay if we do more than kiss." It wasn't like she could get any more pregnant.

"Please fix your shirt."

She gaped at him, his rejection triggering some unwelcome emotions. "Fine." Sitting back in her seat, she righted her shirt and crossed her arms. "If me being pregnant bothers you, then say so."

"It's not that."

"Then what is it?"

"I…" He huffed out a frustrated breath. "I've never done this before."

Her eyes went wide and she blinked then laughed nervously. "You're not a virgin."

She really had no way of knowing if he was or wasn't, but he couldn't be. He was nineteen—and hot. She wasn't the only person having sex at their age. Everyone was doing it, which was why she'd given in when Nick wanted to. It seemed the only way girls could keep a boyfriend—though that didn't really pan out either.

He scoffed. "How would you know?"

"I just…assumed." Wow, maybe she had everything wrong. If she'd known there were guys out there actually capable of waiting she might have been picking out colleges classes instead of strollers. "I'm an idiot. I'm sorry."

"You don't have to apologize." He still sounded irritated.

"Is this, like, a thing? Are you…waiting?"

"I'm not waiting for marriage or anything like that. I just think it should be special. I think people should…be in love."

Her heart pinched as she stared at him. He was a really good guy and sometimes it hurt to know some other girl would end up with him. She took his hand and whispered, "I think that too." She just wished she had thought of it sooner.

From that night on she became obsessed with the phenomenon of love. She wasn't sure how people knew when love was love and not just lust. She never believed she loved Nick or any of her boyfriends before him, but Ant was different. She figured she'd know when he loved her because he'd do more, but maybe he was waiting for her to actually say the words. They were really big words.

As the weeks went on her perspective on men and romance shifted. If not for the thought of him leaving, she never would have rushed things. Ant never made her feel pressured and sometimes kissing was all she really needed. She decided to not think too far into the future and simply trust that the end would eventually come and she'd handle her emotions then. That worked for a while, but not as long as she would have liked.

The morning of graduation she sat on her bed, staring at the floor, wondering why she felt so empty when she'd expected this moment to be the most fulfilling milestone of her life so far. Everyone was so excited to get flung out into the adult world and had so many great prospects ahead of them that she felt apart from her peers. No matter what, she couldn't shake the hollow ache inside of her.

As she donned her gown and pinned her cap in place her mother knocked on her door. "Mum, is this straight?"

"Oh, don't you look lovely." She adjusted her cap and pinched her chin. "I still remember the day I graduated, but mostly I remember looking for your father in the crowd."

Kate sat on the bed and her mother followed. "Did you love him then?"

"Perhaps. Sometimes I think I loved him the first time I set eyes on him. Oh, he had such an arrogant swagger about him. Took my breath away."

Kate smiled, appreciating the special sort of relationship her parents had, and a bit envious, because she might never know the same. "When were you sure you loved him?"

Her mother's head tilted, as she considered the question. "Do you ever get pissed off at someone and your anger crashes over you like a storm?"

Kate thought of Cheryl. "Yes."

"Well, I think loves a bit more subtle. It's like a summer rain that comes and mists everything around you until the world changes colors. Everything's heavier and brighter and a bit messy, but the change is so faint and feels so natural, you hardly realize anything's different at all, but you know you're not the same person you were before that love was born."

"That's really pretty, Mum."

"It's the best I can explain it."

The ache widened like a chasm in her chest, stretching her heart thin. "Do you think I'll ever be in love like you and Daddy?"

"Oh, sweetheart." She clutched her hands, squeezed them affectionately and laughed. "I think you'll know a love a hundred times greater than ours."

"What do you mean?"

"You're having a baby, dearie. There's nothing as strong as a mother's love for her child."

And she was glad for that, but it didn't quite replace the ache inside of her to know the love of a partner. "You're right. I don't know why I'm worrying about this now."

"Is this about Anthony?"

"I don't know. He's leaving in a month and a half and I don't want to make things harder than they already are. I should just be happy that he's been this patient with me so far."

When her mother was quiet, she knew she was holding something back. But she didn't know what it was so she had no way of guessing. "Never mind." Kate stood and checked her reflection one more time.

Her mother stood behind her and rested her hands on her shoulders, her gaze meeting Kate's in the mirror. "You listen to me, Katherine, because no one can make the tough decisions for you. I remember what it was to be your age and to have people tellin' me what could and couldn't be. I didn't always listen, but I did prove to anyone who doubted me that love could overcome extraordinary things. If you love that boy, you love him with all of your heart. And if he loves you, *truly* loves you, it won't matter what came before or what comes next. Love might be subtle, but true love is fierce and not something you'll be wantin' to go up against."

Her heart pinched as she rested her fingers over her mother's. "Thank you—for everything. You and Daddy have been so good about all of this. I could never do it without you."

She kissed her cheek and smiled. "You're our baby girl."

Her mother left her alone and Kate glanced down at her hand. She thought of Anthony and her stomach fluttered with excitement. Pulling off her ring, she turned it and slipped it back onto her finger, crown facing out. Looking at her refection, she smiled and whispered, "Love is subtle."

When they reached the school she proceeded to her place in line and filed through the procession to her future. Kate listened to every word spoken. She hung on the hopes of her class that this *did not* mark an ending, but the start of a new beginning. As she scanned the faces in the crowd, she mentally ticked off those she knew she'd never see again and made amends with those she no longer needed in her life. Of all her classmates, there was only one she wasn't ready to say goodbye to, and as their row stood, McCulloughs to Marcellis, she looked back at him and smiled.

Anthony gave her wink and she took the first step toward her future. Terrified, but also excited for whatever prospects it held.

When she crossed the stage, the principal shook her hand, congratulated her and passed her a diploma. It was all so monumental, but somehow she knew she'd forget this momentary transaction yet always remember the way Anthony smiled and winked at her, giving her the confidence to take that first step.

She watched him accept his diploma, heard his family shout from the bleachers, and smiled as he held it up proudly. He was so charismatic in everything he did, he'd be impossible to ever forget. This was the first of many graduations in his future and he'd worked very hard to earn this moment. They all had.

Once they were back in their row, they waited out the last half of the alphabet until the moment of truth finally came. As one, they lifted their tassels and turned to the next chapter of their lives.

The student body was free and as the audience cheered, Kate searched the crowd and spotted her family already working their way down the bleachers like a stampede of wild caribou. They had a bit to travel, so she searched for Anthony, but his seat was empty much like the rest.

In a sea of blue and white, she tried to find him, but everyone looked the same. For some reason, it became imperative that she see him one last time before he left with his family to go celebrate.

"Katie!"

She turned and searched for him, grinning as he stood on a folding chair waving his cap in the air. She rushed though the students filtering toward the bleachers, apologizing as she shoved her way against the current back into the crowd. He jumped off the chair and she lost sight of him.

"Anthony!"

"Katie!" he yelled back.

Shit. She couldn't find him. The music was so loud and everyone was pushing to go in the opposite direction toward his or her family. "Anthony, where are you?"

A hand closed around her arm and pulled her through the crowd, his voice full of laughter as he whispered in her ear, "I'm right beside you."

She smiled into his dark eyes, the brief rightness of those words becoming something she wished would always be. "We did it."

He pulled her closer, his smile priceless as he cupped her cheeks. "Yeah, we did." His lips pressed to hers as he held her protectively, their bodies, in the rush of caps and gowns, stood as still as a jetty somehow suspended in time.

She hugged him tight as he broke the kiss. His face pressed into her hair and he whispered, "I love you."

A chill stole over her body and then she heard his mother's voice. "Anthony! Where's my boy?"

The crowd was in gridlock, but his mother wedged herself between the bodies to get to her son. Anthony released Kate as his mother barreled toward him, pinching his cheeks hard enough to make Kate wince.

"I'm so proud of you!" She planted a smacking kiss on his cheek and smacked the mark of red lipstick.

"Katie girl!"

Kate turned as her mom and dad approached, McCullough clan in tow. As Ant's sisters and father approached she was bumped toward her family and praised accordingly. There were lots of hugs and kisses from her parents and mostly questions about when they were eating from her siblings.

"Why don't you introduce us to Anthony's family, dearie?"

Kate turned and noted how much noise they made for only being a family of six. The McCulloughs had them beat by three, but the Marcellis had the market cornered on volume. She took her mother's arm and led her to them. Anthony's mother spoke rapidly, her hands swinging wildly in the air as she gestured with every word.

Waiting for a break in the conversation, Kate said, "Mrs. Marcelli, I wanted to introduce you to my mother."

"Oh, my gawd! Let me just hug you." Anthony's mom

pulled Kate's mother into a firm embrace. "What a sweet daughter you have. We just adore Katie. And what a woman you must be to have seven kids! *Marone!* You must be a saint or a sadist, either way I already like you."

Her mother beamed with pride. "Well, I don't know if I'm anything close to a saint, but I do keep close ties with Tully and Jameson for the pain. And I'm never out of reach of a wooden spoon, if you catch my drift."

"Do I ever." Anthony's mother rolled her eyes and waved her hand. "I got three teenage girls."

"Well, I'll tell you, boys are no picnic either. My twins, I'd like to beat them something fierce. They're nothing like your Anthony. What a darling he is."

Mrs. Marcelli preened and yanked her son closer, mushing his cheek with another smacking kiss. "Isn't he! Oh, I could cry I'm so proud of him."

Anthony stumbled to Kate's side the moment his mother released him. "This might be a match made in heaven," he mumbled out the side of his mouth.

She laughed nervously, unable to think of anything other than what he'd whispered in her ear just before they were interrupted. Maybe he was just excited and not thinking.

"Frank! Let's all go to O'Malley's for dinner. The Marcellis are joining us," her mother announced.

Kate smiled up at Ant. His family might be the loudest here, but once the aunts were involved the Marcellis didn't stand a chance of getting a word in edgewise. "Can I ride with you?"

"Of course." He took her hand, already leading her out of the crowd. Looking back he yelled, "Ma! We'll meet you there. Katie and I are driving over together."

"Okay, you two be good. We'll see you in a few!" She turned back to Kate's mother, hardly yelling but loud enough to be heard. "Aren't they adorable. Oh, to be that in love."

There was that word again. It wouldn't stop echoing in her ears. When they got to the car she was uncharacteristically nervous.

"You're quiet," he said, as they reached the road.

"I'm just thinking."

"It's pretty crazy. We're finally done. It's a little surreal."

Realizing he was speaking about graduating, she again wondered if he was even aware of what he'd said. She wanted to ask, but something held her back.

When they reached O'Malley's a dreadful thought occurred. Anthony's parents had no idea she was pregnant and her aunts circulated more news than the *Dailey Bugle*. Anxious to get them alone and beg them not to mention the baby, she rushed out of the car.

"Hey, slow down," Anthony called.

"I have to use the bathroom." It wasn't a lie, but she also had to find her aunts.

As soon as she reached the inside of the bar the crowd took her breath away. She should have realized they wouldn't be the only families going there after graduation.

Spotting her Aunt Colleen behind the bar, she headed that way.

"Hey, Katie! How's it feel to be free?" her aunt cheerfully greeted.

"Can I talk to you for a minute—in the back?"

Colleen glanced at her and finished mixing a drink before passing it to one of the waitresses. "We gotta make it quick. I have a full house."

"Where's Aunt Rose?"

Colleen scanned the bar and grinned. "There she is, finding a seat for your mother."

Her heart raced. There wasn't enough time for privacy. Grabbing her aunt's arm she squeezed and whispered, "She can't say anything about the baby, Aunt Colleen. Anthony's parents don't know I'm pregnant."

Colleen's eyes widened and she understood how fast they'd have to move to intercept her sister's big mouth. "Oh dear. Okay, you go sit with the others. I'll handle it."

Kate nodded and quickly took a detour to the restroom, trusting her Aunt Colleen to do whatever it took to lock up Aunt Rosemarie's gob. As she worked her way back through the bar toward the tables her nerves finally calmed. But then she saw her aunt's face. It was too late.

Kate's steps faltered as she registered every set of Marcelli eyes staring at her. Colleen walked over to her and took her hands. "I'm sorry, love. I tried."

Rosemarie glanced over the crowd, her eyes heavy with regret, but Kate was more focused on the look of shock twisting Anthony's mother's face. His dad wore a different expression, one full of disappointment.

Her feet weighed heavily on the floor as she faced their judgment. She desperately searched for the sense of adoration she'd known from these people just moments ago, but it was gone. Her gaze found Anthony's and she stilled, not sure if she'd ever seen him look at her in such a way.

Pulling his chair back from the table, he stood. His smile was a slow comfort that anchored her. Taking his time, he rounded the table and came to her side, sliding his fingers into hers before facing the others. "Let's put other issues aside for the day and focus on celebrating one milestone at a time."

It was as if his maturity was doubled the moment they graduated, because he addressed them with absolute authority and the unflinching confidence of a grown man. His mother's lips parted as her brow creased. His father shook his head and his sisters gawked. "Anthony, when did this happen?" his father demanded.

Kate's chest tightened. They couldn't take this out on him. It was her responsibility. Anthony was just her friend. Then she considered the protective way he stood beside her and it clicked. His father was making the same assumption her father had. "It's not—"

"We'll discuss it later," Anthony spoke over her, squeezing her hand.

Kate looked to her family, finding her father frowning and her mother pursing her lips and hiding a smug smile.

She couldn't let him worry his parents over someone else's troubles. It wasn't right and it would spoil what was an otherwise perfect day for them.

Anthony stepped toward the table and she tugged him back, her eyes pleading. "Anthony, tell them the truth. It's fine," she whispered.

He turned his back to the others and looked into her eyes. "It's none of their business, Kate. Let them think what they will. I'll not have anyone judging you—even my family."

Her vision blurred as she stared at him, wondering why he would take the heat for someone else's mistake. She shook her head as her mother's words came back to her. Everything was suddenly heavier inside of her, messy, but the same. She finally understood the subtle ache of love.

Overwhelmed, she glanced at the others and dashed a tear from her eye. She couldn't do this in front of them. "We'll be back in a minute."

She tugged him through the bar and out the back door. When her feet reached the pavement, she turned on him. "Why did you do that?"

He shrugged. "Why should anyone feel like they can judge you?"

"But it's not yours. You made them think the baby's yours."

He glanced away, his expression hiding something. "Anthony."

Shaking his head, he said, "Maybe I'm not ready for them to know it's not."

"What? Why?"

Again he shrugged. "Because they wouldn't understand." He gazed into her eyes, brow tight with stress. "I love you, Kate. I don't care if other people don't get it or think it's too complicated. It's how I feel and the only person's opinion I want on the matter is yours."

Swallowing tightly, she felt the words fighting to come out, but she couldn't let him take this sort of fall for her. It would cause more problems, because he'd eventually have to tell them the truth. "Don't love me, Anthony."

He took her hands, holding her fingers tight as he whispered, "Too late."

Her tears slipped past her lashes as she shut her eyes. "You can't lead them to believe this is your situation. It's mine. I appreciate you trying to protect me, but you need to look out for yourself. It's graduation day. Your parents are so proud of you and happy for your future. Don't take that away from them, even if just for a minute." She met his stare, putting so much of her heart on the line, and said, "You have to go tell them the baby's not yours. Tell them nothing's changed."

His lips pressed tight. "What's so wrong with letting people think it's mine, Kate?"

"Everything." She staggered back. "My God, Anthony, do you hear how crazy you sound?"

"Why is it crazy? We're dating. Shit happens. How is having a fatherless child better than what I'm suggesting?"

"Because you're not the father! This doesn't fix anything. It just hurts your parents."

"I don't care."

"Well, I do. I like your family and I don't want to hurt them. I'm going to tell them the truth." Turning toward the door, she took a step and he caught her arm, pulling her toward him and cupping her shoulders. His eyes held such intensity she shook under his gaze.

"Do you love me? I love you, Kate. It isn't going to go away in two months just because I have to go to college. This isn't something temporary for me."

"But it has to be! That's what we said it would be."

"I don't care what we said. Every day I love you more than the last. It's insane to think at the end of summer we'll just be able to shut off our feelings and move on. I don't want to move on without you. I want us to stay together."

"But you're leaving."

"So what? People have long distance relationships all the time."

Her lips trembled as she tried so hard not to fall into the trap of hoping this could be more. She was so afraid to trust his words, unsure if they'd be true once he actually moved to campus and met so many others like himself. "Even if we don't break up, you can't lead them to believe—"

"What if we get married?"

"*What?*" Now she was really worried he'd lost his mind. "Anthony, we're kids."

"We're adults, Katherine. I'm not saying now, but what if it eventually happens? Do you honestly think I'd treat this child any different than our other children? Nick isn't here. I'm here. Don't burn bridges before we've crossed them."

Blinking, she looked up at the sky. "You don't have to lie to your family."

"I'm not lying. I'm…avoiding the truth—at least for a little while until we see where things go."

Shutting her eyes, she winced, recalling the palpable judgment inside. "I hate the way they looked at me. It's like everything's suddenly different. They'll resent me for that, because they think this will affect you."

His hands moved to her face as he pressed his forehead to hers. "Not if I take my fair share. Let me share the load, Kate. It's what good men do. Let them look. Nothing is changing how I feel about you. You're mine and, no matter how different things feel, that's something that isn't changing. I love you."

Sniffling, she met his stare. "I love you too, Anthony. I just wish I'd met you before—"

His lips silenced her confession. His arms wrapped around her, holding her tight. "You don't have to wish anything. We're here now and this is exactly where I want to be. Understand?"

Not really, but she nodded anyway. Taking a deep breath, she released a shaky sigh. "It's going to be hard going back in there."

"Then let's go somewhere else."

"We can't do that." But it was exactly what she wanted to do. She wanted to escape and run away with him, hide someplace the rest of the world couldn't reach them. At least for a little while.

The back door opened and they turned as Colleen stilled. "I didn't realize anyone was out here." She lifted a bag of trash. "I was just running this to the dumpster."

It was clear she felt guilty for not intercepting Rosemarie soon enough, but it wasn't her fault. "We were just talking," Kate told her.

Colleen hoisted the trash into the bin and brushed off her hands. "That was a ballsy thing you did in there, Anthony, taking the heat off Katie like you did."

He shrugged. "It seemed like the right thing to do."

Colleen smiled, her gaze drifting between the two of them. "Aye." She hesitated a moment, then glanced at the door. "I'm guessing they'll ask me if I saw you on my travels out here." She raised her brows. "I could easily tell them I didn't, being that my vision isn't what it used to be."

Anthony glanced at Kate and a sense of urgency stole over her, causing her heart to race. This was why, for all their trouble, she loved her family regardless.

Colleen winked and reached into her apron, pulling out a wad of tips. "Go have fun and celebrate. Today's an important day for you two."

Kate hesitated, but her aunt forced the money into her hand.

"Go on, now, before someone else comes searching for you."

"Thanks, Aunt Col."

"Don't mention it. Now, get."

When her aunt disappeared into the bar, Anthony looked at her and laughed. "She's the coolest aunt ever."

She nodded. "She has her moments. But she's right. We better go before someone else comes looking for us."

He grinned and took her hand. "Let's go."

They raced back to the car and fled the bar. They had no idea where they were going or how long they'd be gone. They just knew they were on their way to something great and they were moving forward together.

CHAPTER 11

They'd driven for hours, stopped for a bite to eat and filled the car with gas only to drive some more. Anthony had no idea where they were, and the further they drove the more rural the roads became, but he wondered what would happen if they stopped. Not worried. He wasn't quite sure what he was feeling.

"It's getting dark," Kate whispered beside him.

"Do you want to go back?" He'd have a lot to answer for, but no part of him planned on backpedaling.

"No."

He glanced at her and back to the road. "I think we're almost to New York."

"What if we never went back?"

"Kate." They had to go back. As much as he loved leaving everything behind for a bit, their parents were likely freaking out. He couldn't imagine what his mom and dad had said after they disappeared, but he didn't think it was great.

Strangely, he had no regrets about misleading them where the baby was concerned. He had extreme anxiety, sure, but no regrets. He loved her. He was certain of it. Sometime over the past few weeks he'd stopped planning for tomorrow and reached further into his future, imagining what their home would someday look like, how many children they'd have together.

He didn't intend to acquire that future by skulking around and denying what it was he was after. "We can't run away forever."

She shifted in her seat, counting the money her aunt had given them. "There's over a hundred bucks here. We could get a motel room."

A chill raced through his body, his grip tightening on the wheel. "We could do that." His heart beat quickly. Would they be sleeping in different beds? "Did you want to do that?"

"Do you?"

He couldn't seem to catch his breath, but he thought he appeared remarkably calm on the outside, which was good. "Sure."

They drove a while longer and found a little motel just as the sun set. Seventy-four dollars later and they were handed a key. They walked in silence to room Eight and his hands slightly trembled as he unlocked the door. It wasn't paradise. It was a shabby little room with olive carpet and brown curtains. And a bed. There was definitely a bed. They stepped inside and stared at the comforter.

"I'm going to go get some ice and see if I can find a vending machine," Kate announced.

"Okay." He was relieved to have a minute to himself.

As soon as she left he went into the bathroom and stared at his reflection, waiting for some sort of epiphany to come. The sound of the motel door opened and he realized he'd been standing there for five minutes.

"Ant?"

"I'm in the bathroom. I'll be out in a minute." Reaching in his pocket he removed his wallet and dug out the condom he carried. Then stuffed it back in his pocket. Taking a deep breath, he opened the bathroom the door and—Sweet Jesus.

Kate sat on the bed, under the covers. Her bare shoulders showed and the lights were dim. "I couldn't find an ice machine, but I got two sodas."

He swallowed. Maybe they were just going to sleep. Nodding, he shuffled toward the other side of the bed then back to the dresser. "Okay. Thanks."

Turning his back, he slowly unbuttoned his shirt and slipped it off his shoulders, resting it on the arm of the chair. His fingers went to the button of his pants and he hesitated. Better to keep his pants on. His gaze drifted to the folded pile of Kate's clothes on the dresser and his heart pounded faster.

He wanted to be with her, never wanted anything more, but he also wanted everything to be just right.

Clearing his throat, he turned and faced the bed. God, she was beautiful. He took a small step forward. "Are you tired?"

"Not really," she said. "Are you?"

Swallowing again, he shook his head. "No."

Her smile was gentle and a touch unsure. Taking a deep breath, he rounded the bed and slid beside her, under the covers. She laid back on the pillows so he did the same, both of them staring at the ceiling.

Her hand reached for his under the blanket and squeezed. "Is this okay?"

He turned to his side, close enough to count the sparse freckles dotting her nose. "Are you sure about this, Kate?"

She smiled again and nodded. "I love you, Anthony."

Relief came with a deep breath as contentment filled him. This was right. "I love you too."

Leaning close, he brushed his lips to hers and her fingers teased softly through his hair, sending chills down his spine. Pulling back slowly, he whispered, "Can I look at you?"

She nodded and he gently lowered the covers. His breath stilled in his chest. She was so damn perfect. Her porcelain skin flushed as the tips of her rosy breasts tightened into delectable little peaks. "You're so pretty, Katie."

Her smile was shy, but trusting. "You can touch me."

He lifted his hand, hesitating for a final second, unsure how to touch someone so beautiful. His fingers gently lowered, tracing her shoulder and gradually dropped to her breast. When he brushed his thumb over her nipple she drew in a sharp breath, her chest pressing into his touch. Leaning down, he kissed her milky skin and she moaned. The sweet sound crawled into him, wreaking havoc on his heart.

Her fingers pulled him closer, sifting through his hair and down to his back as he pulled the tight tip of her breast into his mouth. Rolling over her, he stilled, careful not to put too much weight on her. His gaze drifted lower and he saw the slightest swell at her abdomen.

Looking into her eyes, he eased down and kissed her. With every caress of her fingers his body came alive. Their mouths teased as his hands gently explored her curves. Little sighs filled the room, drawing his senses to life and soon he was rocking over her, breathing jaggedly, his body begging for more.

Pushing the blankets away, he slid down her body, placing gentle kisses on her breasts and hips. Her tapered legs shifted the lower he moved and there was no resistance as he nudged her thighs apart. His fingers teased her sex, sliding through her arousal and gliding into her by the slightest degree. The heat of her channel coated his seeking fingers, dragging his mind to a place of no return.

She moaned and spread her legs wider, her face tipping back as he pleasured her slowly. Inching down the mattress, he kissed her thighs and fit his shoulders between her legs. She was perfect there too. Keeping his touch light, he pressed his tongue into her and she gasped.

He teased her folds, kissing and caressing and soon she was panting and breathlessly repeating his name. Then she did something incredible. Her body shivered as her fingers curled into the blankets and she arched into him. Her cries pitched as she softly pleaded that it was too much and not enough. He closed his lips around her sensitive clit as his fingers pressed deep, driving her over the edge again and again.

As her strength waned her body settled into the mattress and she sighed. He cradled her in his arms, nipping her shoulders with soft kisses. "I've never felt anything like that," she whispered, a telling blush on her cheeks. Her fingers brushed the button of his pants. "Take these off."

Reaching between them, he loosened his pants and slid them off his legs. She nestled into him, her mouth pressing sweet kisses onto his chest as her hand traveled down his stomach.

He sucked in a breath as she cupped him through his shorts, her touch firm and intoxicating. Driven by a burst of desire, he turned her face and kissed her deeply. Her fingers pressed into the material of his shorts, curled around his length, pulling and teasing him to the point of insanity.

The moment she slid her hand behind the fabric and caught his flesh in her palm the pleasure nearly choked him. "Jesus, Kate." There was no catching his breath.

Holding him tight, she stroked him until he could barely hold off his release. He caught her wrist and kissed her, slowly thrusting into her palm. "Are you ready?"

She nodded and eased back as he reached for his pants.

His hands trembled as he slid the condom over his flesh. Fitting his body over hers, he looked into her eyes. "I never want you to forget this moment, Kate. Nothing that came before matters."

She brushed her lips softly over his. "I'll never forget this moment as long as I live, Anthony."

He pressed into her and shut his eyes. Tight heat encased him as he took a second to process just how incredible her body fit with his. Perfect.

Watching her through his lashes, he whispered, "I love you. No matter what happens, you'll always be my first love."

"And you'll always be mine."

ON THE DRIVE home Ant made several decisions, but he kept them to himself. First, he had no intention of breaking up with Kate, for college or any other reason. Two, he wasn't telling his parents the truth about the baby. He might be a naïve man, but right now he saw no feasible reason why they couldn't make this work.

Kate was an honest person, and so was he, for the most part, but maintaining the illusion that the baby was his would benefit them in the end. Something told him this was protecting not only Kate, but her child as well. It seemed the honorable thing to do and he wanted to be the man to do it.

As they reached the McCullough's property he smiled

at her, thinking her even more beautiful than just a minute ago. "How much trouble do you think you'll be in?"

She shrugged. "We're adults. They'll be mad I didn't call, but there really isn't anything they can do."

She was right, but even he knew he'd be walking into a shitstorm. "Do you have any regrets?"

Her smile was one he'd always remember, full of secrets they shared. No longer were there secrets that divided them. "Not a single one."

He reached for her hand and pressed a kiss to the backs of her fingers. "Me neither."

When he dropped her off he promised he'd be back in a few hours. That seemed the maximum time he could go without seeing her before his mind went mad with missing her. August was sure to kill him when he left for school.

Once he was alone in the car, his nerves got the better of him. His parents would have a hundred questions and he wasn't sure if he knew which answers to give. As he parked in the driveway he took a galvanizing breath and prayed whatever he walked into wasn't as bad as he imagined.

Stepping into the kitchen, he paused. His mother was at the table clipping coupons and her eyes briefly met his then her gaze shifted away, her head lowering and hiding her expression.

"Hey, Ma."

"Anthony." Her greeting was clipped as she sliced her

good sheers through the sales ads.

He slid his keys on the counter. "Where's Dad?"

"Sleeping on the couch."

"Oh." Sleeping sounded like a great idea since he hadn't had much the night before, staying up until the sun rose with Kate and learning all the many facets of her. It was the best night of his life and he'd never felt so complete, so certain that she was the one. "I'm going to go—"

"Have a seat."

Right. He slid into the chair and eyed the scissors as she set them on the table, wishing they weren't there.

Her lips slightly trembled, but she contained her emotions well. "Do you have something to say to me?"

"I'm sorry about yesterday."

Her mouth pursed and she leveled him with a withering look only mothers seemed capable of making. "Do you love this girl, Anthony?"

His chest seemed to ripple with all the affection he held and his answer came in a rasp. "Very much."

She continued to study him for a long minute. The longer she scrutinized him the more he recalled how hard it was to deceive the woman that gave birth to him. Somehow, she always got the truth out of him. It was like she had some sort of crystal ball. But he held strong. He'd made up his mind and he was keeping his vow. This was between him and Kate. Nothing else mattered.

Finally, she said, "It's trash night. Take the cans to the curb before you do anything else."

What? He wasn't one to look a gift horse in the mouth,

so he wasn't going to argue. If the trash cans were her greatest concern at the moment, then so be it. Relieved, he hesitantly rose from the table. "I'll take them down now."

As soon as he reached the door, she said, "And Anthony?"

He stilled. He knew that was too easy. "Yeah, Ma?"

"You *are* going to college."

He silently chuckled. "I know, Ma." Realizing she was doing her best to accept the situation, he walked back to the table and kissed her head. "I love you, Ma."

She lightly patted his cheek. "You better. Your father was a maniac last night. So long as we're clear that this will not change your immediate plans, we'll figure everything else out. Now go take care of the trash."

CHAPTER 12

Kate entered the kitchen and hesitated at the sight of her mother. "Hi, Mum."

Turning from the sink, she eyed her from head to toe. "You look well."

Nervously, Kate approached the counter and picked up a cloth to dry the dishes as they were washed. "I feel okay."

"Oh, I'd thought you'd feel a bit more than okay."

"I'm sorry I left last night, Mum. I was embarrassed."

Her mother sighed. "You better get a thicker skin, love. Children don't leave much room for mortification. Pretty soon you'll be pissing with the door wide open and talking to yourself like a regular old nutcase. Motherhood does that to a person."

She frowned, not expecting this casual welcome. "Aren't you mad?"

Her mom glanced at her and smirked. "What good

would that do? Colleen told me what happened. She said she gave you money and I figured after everything Anthony did, you'd be wanting to spend some time alone to figure things out…and other things."

The tension in her shoulders loosened.

"You're a good girl, Katherine. Got yourself into some trouble this one time, but I know you're not the sort to go lookin' for more. You're an adult, soon to be a mother, I think the best thing to do is start lettin' you decide what's best for yourself."

Kate laughed, a bit outside of her senses, and wondered if her mother was always this cool or if this was something that came with age. "Thanks for understanding."

She shut off the faucet and faced her, her vibrant green eyes serious. "That boy lied for you last night, Katherine."

"I didn't ask him to."

"I know." She pulled her to the table and they sat down. "There aren't a lot of men that would chance their honor for the honor of someone else. Your father and I were impressed, to say the least."

She didn't want them getting ahead of themselves. "I told him to tell his parents the truth."

Her mother cocked her head to the side. "We'll see if that's necessary. He obviously cares very deeply for you. I say, let him do this for you. If anything changes, he knows you aren't the sort of person to cause others harm."

Her heart pinched. "He can't take responsibility for something he didn't do."

Leaning over the table her mother whispered, "But maybe he wishes he had done it."

Kate rolled her eyes. "Mum, he's going to college. His life's just beginning. Trust me, he's not wishing for this."

She patted her hands. "Well, for what it's worth, Anthony has won over your parents and we hope you keep him around."

He'd won her over too, so much so, she worried how she'd ever live without him in her days. "I'm going to take a nap for a while."

"Okay, love. I'll call you when supper's ready."

When she reached her room she didn't sleep, despite her exhaustion. She studied her room and slowly unpinned keepsakes from her wall. When she had all her childhood memories packed away, she sat on the bed and stared at the blank space. Maybe she should paint?

Something had changed over the past twenty-four hours. The tension that came with school had disappeared and in its absence, Kate realized just how much school had been weighing on her, how great the relief of freedom was.

She'd spent her entire life preparing, that's what kids did, of course. They prepared for kindergarten, then moved on the middle-school. Each benchmark came with unknown expectations and the anticipation that eventually life would begin. Going to high school had been the highlight of her life. She'd embarked on endless possibilities, and entered a world of new freedoms. Sometimes she forgot to think about all the tomorrows and how one snap decision could change everything. She wasn't so forgetful anymore.

When she started her senior year there came an immense pressure to be *something*. Her friends somehow identified fields that fit their futures with a certainty she didn't share. Even Ant had somehow, after years of playing sports, figured out he wanted to work in the medical field. If she looked at her collective past, nothing truly jumped out at her as a special talent.

Her years played back like pictures of a children's book, fluttering too fast for her to truly see all that hid on each page. She couldn't quite recall a time before Colin. And then came the twins. They were all so different and she wondered what sort of child her baby would be, allowing herself to embrace the excitement that slipped in behind the wonder.

While Luke was wild, Finn was refined. Braydon was an angel, the timing of his birth perfect, as she was still young, but wanted to be mature and still play house. She was enamored by him, and couldn't recall ever loving someone more. Her worry mimicked her mother's and the first time he'd skinned his knee she was sickened with dread, hovering over him for days so he wouldn't get hurt again. But he did.

There were scrapes and bruises and once Kelly came along, endless bickering and boyish battles. Sheilagh was a surprise, as she suspected her mother didn't have any girl genes left to give. She was so dainty compared to her little brother and Kate desperately wanted to put braids and bows in her hair, but Sheilagh was a little devil and would rip them out and race after her brothers, determined to keep pace, proving whatever boys could do she could manage just as well.

If she knew anything about children, and thinking back, she knew a lot, she knew each child was unique and special. Somehow, removing the clutter of her past, meaningless relics that told the story of a girl and nothing of the woman, made it easier to see the future. She wanted to be everything for her baby—the hero her dad would always be and the well of endless nurturing her mother provided.

Her hand rested on her belly as she smiled, truly letting her happiness settle and take shape in a way she hadn't thus far. This was *her* baby and she already felt like a mother. The void that widened as her peers recognized their callings slowly filled with love. A sense of peace settled over her, leaving no room for the regret that once had been.

"Kate?" Her brother, Colin, knocked on her door and stepped in. "Can I take your car into town? My headlight's out and it's getting dark."

"Sure. Keys are on the counter."

He glanced around her room. "It's so empty in here."

She smiled at the boxes on the floor, their presence emphasizing her certainty that she was ready to move on. "I'm trying to make room for new things."

He grinned, blue eyes soft as he stared at her. "You're starting to show."

Colin would be next to leave, and then the twins and Braydon, and one day this big old house would be empty after they all moved on. Strange that she might be the last to truly leave.

Her eyes took him in, such a constant presence in her days. "I'm going to miss you when you're gone." Knowing her brother, he'd travel farthest of all. Colin's goals were slightly different than most kids his age.

"Mum's upset with me. She keeps pushing other colleges at me, but…"

"You know what you want." The first time Colin announced he'd wanted to dedicate his life to God she'd thought he'd change his mind—they all did. But over the last few years his dedication only grew.

He quietly laughed, a touch unsure. "I wish there were guarantees in life, but sometimes there's only faith. I think this is right for me." His attention returned to her stomach. "But you make me question how much I'll truly be giving up."

"Me?"

He nodded, his eyes uncertain. "I never thought of us having kids until you were in this situation. I guess that's silly. Eventually, you'll all have families, even Sheilagh."

"You'll have a family too. You'll have us."

His lips pursed. "But I'll never have what you'll have. Envy's a tough thing to handle and I don't know if it'll fade with time."

How strange to think her brother might envy her situation. But knowing he'd become a priest and never know what it is to be a parent, made her sad, once again delivering a heap of gratitude to her heart. She rested her hand over her belly. "I'm happy."

He met her gaze and smiled. "And I'm happy for you. You're going to make an incredible mum."

When Colin left she made a list of items she wanted for her room. In a sense, she believed she was redoing her life. Though she didn't know how much baby clothes or diapers cost, she guessed and estimated what sort of price tag her future would hold. At first it seemed affordable, but as each little item added up so did the pressure.

Taking her list, she went downstairs to find her father. "Dad?"

He looked up from the television. "Is it time to eat?"

"No." She sat beside him on the couch, her fingers holding her list tight. "Can I start work tomorrow?"

His brow lifted. "Do you need money for something?"

"Dad, come on."

"You can start, but I want you to keep looking for something better. It's not a glamorous job, sweetheart."

She sighed, more of the weight taken off of her shoulders. "Thank you, Daddy."

"What do you got there?"

Her hands folded the list. "Nothing. Just a list of things I'm going to need."

He took the paper from her and scanned over it before passing it back. "Tomorrow is actually a good day to start. I have an appointment in the morning, so I won't be around. Estelle will be busy so you can help with the phones when she's tied up."

Kate smiled, glad to know she was actually needed in the office and not just a charity case. "I'll do my best."

"I'm sure you will."

THE FOLLOWING day was exhausting and exhilarating. Her father wasn't lying when he said his secretary would be extra busy in his absence. Thankfully, Estelle was very patient and didn't flip out when Kate fought with the fax machine—for the tenth time.

"It's not typically like this," Estelle reminded. "Your father usually plans ahead when he's out and everyone has an idea of what they should be doing. Today they're all just running around like a bunch of chickens with their heads chopped off."

Kate barely had a chance to eat her lunch. Every time she took a bite the phones rang, but she absolutely loved it. No matter how many debacles she came across, she knew she was doing something productive for her future and that came with great pride.

The ride back to the house was made with a smile. Ant was coming over for dinner and she was anxious to talk to him about his first day, too. He never did come back to the lumberyard for a job. She supposed one trauma was enough. But he was smart and had no problem finding work at the hardware store in town. She was eager to hear about his first day and hoped it was as exhilarating as hers.

As she entered the house her mom and dad were sitting at the table. "How was your first day in the workforce, Katie girl?"

She put her lunch pail on the counter and grinned. "I didn't ruin anything, so I'd say it was a success."

Her dad smiled. "Was Estelle helpful?"

"When she could be. Things were a little hectic, but she said that's not the norm. How was your meeting?"

"Good." He looked at her mother who was being uncharacteristically quiet.

"Well, I'm going to change. These pants are cutting into my hips."

They both nodded. Something was off. Taking the steps, she mentally planned out what to wear to work tomorrow, thinking some elastic slacks were in her near future. She turned into her bedroom and stilled in the doorway.

Her lips parted as she immediately noticed all the new additions. The old changing table was in the corner and stacked full of diapers. The crib from the attic sat beside it, clean and wearing a fresh coat of paint. Her mother's rocker was also there.

Taking a staggering step across the threshold, she drew in a stuttering breath and picked up a tiny rattle resting on her bed. The handle had a bow tied out of rope. She knew that rope. It was the twine her father always kept in his pocket when they walked the property so he could make a quick mend if a fencepost was down.

She slowly pivoted and blinked back tears, taking inventory of all he'd done. This was where he was today, not at a meeting, but here, doing this for her and her baby. She looked inside the basket on the floor and found it packed with tiny articles of clothing. Picking up the little set of mint and lemon yellow booties, she smiled through her tears.

"I figured getting that list checked off might help."

She twisted and faced her dad, his large form filling her doorway as he leaned on the jamb. She couldn't think of anything to say. Thank you didn't seem enough and at the moment her throat was so tight she wasn't sure she could get a word out.

Wiping her cheeks, she walked to him and flung her arms around him, squeezing with all her might. There was no fear she might hurt him. He was strong, hero strong, and he could take it.

"I love you," she rasped as he tightened his arms around her and kissed her head.

"Love you too, Katie girl."

Pulling back, she wiped her eyes again and laughed. "I'll be crying all night now."

He chuckled. "That's okay. Your mother had seven kids. I've seen enough pregnancy tears to fill a small river. I'm used to it."

She laughed again. "Thank you for this. It's… I can't even tell you how much it means to me, not just the things, but how supportive you and Mum are being with everything."

He smiled softly, his eyes creasing with true affection. "That's what family does. You're my little girl. I'll always do whatever I can for you."

"Thank you, Daddy."

That night, when Anthony came over, she showed him everything her parents had done. He stilled in the doorway, taken aback by all the changes.

"Wow." His gaze made a slow revolution around the room and he grinned. Stepping to the basket of diapers, he lifted one, making it appear even smaller in his large hand. "These are so tiny."

"They're for newborns. I have ones for when he or she gets bigger, too."

"They got you everything."

It was surreal to see all these items in living color, to touch them and smell the soft scent of each delicate piece. "It sure does make everything real."

He glanced over his shoulder, a peculiar look in his eye as his mouth curved into a content grin. "It really does."

Scared yet? The words almost came out, but she held them back. Nothing in the way he touched the baby items or admired the crib showed any sign of intimidation. He put the diaper back in the basket and turned the rocker to face the bed. Lowering himself into the chair, he folded his hands between his knees and smiled at her.

"I can picture you," he said quietly, glancing at the

changing table. "It's weird. I can actually see you using all of these things."

She was still working on that, but being surrounded by so many reminders helped. "It's going to be strange, always having to put someone else before myself."

"You do that anyway. It's the kind of girl you are."

She'd done that with him. It was why she tried to spare him from her chaos. For the briefest moment she imagined what these items might look like in a house of her own, with Anthony's belongings scattered in between.

He stared off, his attention focused on the crib.

ANT COULDN'T BELIEVE how different her room looked. Everything had changed in the blink of an eye. Little items washed their world in pastels, seeming like luxuries, but these were the necessities of her future. Their future.

He wasn't prepared for the surge of emotion seeing these items had brought. It was a mixture of comfort and longing. He didn't know Kate before the baby. They'd always been two, he being the person that made them three. When he thought of her, touched her, he never forgot all that she was, and that was who he loved—all of her.

His eyes burned with the unfamiliar sensation of tears and he blinked hard to hide them away. He loved them both, her, and her unborn child. And never had he wished for a sense of entitlement as much as he did in that moment.

Reaching across the space, he caught her fingers in his and squeezed. He'd thought to tell her of his day and ask about hers, but now, that all seemed so trivial in the grand scheme of things. "I love you."

Her smile gentled as she looked into his eyes. "I love you too."

If only she understood how much. Eventually she'd have to accept that his feelings for her didn't come with limits and encompassed *all* of her, the woman she was, the child she carried, and the future she'd face. He wanted that future with her. This was just another sign that he was exactly where he was meant to be.

As the weeks unfolded into summer, Kate fell into a sort of routine. Most nights Anthony came to her house and some nights she went to his. His sisters had lots of questions about pregnancy, but his father never made a peep whenever the baby came into conversation. His mother was a little different. She was constantly slipping little trinkets of luck into Kate's hands and tying red ribbons on her clothes, saying something about red keeping the *Mallocchios* away. Kate wasn't very superstitious, but it seemed like a good idea to take all the good luck charms she could get.

On the weekends she spent time with her mother,

learning how to knit and together they worked on blankets and sweaters for the baby. The mountain got cold in the winter, which was when her baby was due, so she never stopped adding to her supply of warm clothing.

Anthony often stuck around, but busied himself helping her dad fix things that needed fixing around the house. Anthony truly stole her mother's heart the day he convinced her dad to finally fix the stove.

When Kate's second trimester rolled around, she was excited to have her sonogram. Her mother was joining her, which she thought was normal in her case, until she spoke to Anthony the night before.

"Can I go?" he asked as they sat on the porch after dinner.

"You have work."

"But I could leave for an hour. This is important, Kate."

It was important, but not necessarily important to *his* life. Yet, somehow he acted like her baby held every bit of significance in his world, as it did in hers. "If you want to be there, I don't mind. But I'd understand if you weren't."

"I'll pick you up at eleven."

And so it was settled. As she waited in the kitchen for Ant to come pick them up her mother, wearing cleaning clothes, dragged out the mop and bucket.

"Mum, we have to leave soon. What are you doing? Anthony's going to be here any minute."

"I'm mopping this floor."

"But my appointment's in twenty minutes."

"I know, dearie. But this is something for you and

Anthony. I'm excited for you, but I don't want to intrude on that private moment."

She frowned. "But I want you there."

"Trust me on this, Katherine. The person who should be there *will* be there."

Just then a horn honked out front. Kate stared at her mother as the door opened and Anthony stepped into the kitchen. "You ready?"

She glanced at him and back to her mother, feeling like a little kid being permitted to cross the street alone for the first time. She collected her purse and the little appointment book the doctor's office gave her. "You're sure you don't want to come?"

Her mother nodded. "I'm sure. You bring me back a picture of my grandchild. Go on. You don't want to be late."

Once they were in the car and on their way, Anthony took her hand. "You excited?"

"Excited. Nervous. I just hope everything's okay and the baby's healthy."

"I'm sure everything will be great." He squeezed her hand.

Once they signed in at the doctor's office they were shown to a room in the back. Kate changed into a patient gown and waited on the examination table as Ant scoped out the room. She was a little self-conscious about being so exposed in front of him, but he never acted like he couldn't handle it. Strange that this was the second time he'd see her anything close to naked. As far as second dates went, this wasn't what she had in mind.

The doctor came in and asked her several questions. He introduced himself to Anthony and told him exactly where to stand so he could see the baby on the screen. Once they were caught up, she reclined on the table and covered her legs with a paper blanket. The doctor parted her gown and slathered her belly with cool gel.

She glanced nervously at Ant who smiled back and whispered, "You're really starting to show."

She supposed there was a big difference between now and graduation night, but he didn't seem bothered by the changes to her body.

The screen flipped on and their attention turned to the doctor. "There we go."

Her breath pulled deep, filling her lungs and sending chills down her arms. "Wow."

"Look at that," Ant said, mesmerized. "That's incredible."

Without thinking, she blindly reached for his hands and his fingers entwined with hers. Using her free hand, she wiped away a tear.

"Did you want to know the sex?" the doctor asked.

"It's a boy," she rasped. She didn't have any science to base her theory on, but she had such a strong instinct she was looking at her son.

The doctor chuckled and moved the arrow to show them the proof. "Right you are."

"Oh my God," Anthony whispered, his hand squeezing a little tighter. "You're having a boy, Katie."

She glanced at him and smiled when she saw the sheen of tears shimmering over his dark eyes. His gaze shifted to her and his smile widened. "That's your son," he whispered, voice hoarse.

Holding on to her overwhelming emotions by a thread, she murmured, "I love you." Her mother was right. The person who needed to be here for this moment was right by her side.

They spent the next thirty minutes going over the images and discussing the baby's general health, which seemed to be fine. Everything was developing on schedule and her due date was early December. Although she had over four months to go, it seemed only moments away.

When they got back to the house her mother gushed over the images the doctor had printed for them. Though they weren't the easiest to read, Kate loved that little blob in those pictures more than she ever thought she could love anything.

"I have to go back to work," Anthony said after her mother force-fed them lunch.

She wanted to tell him so much in that moment but lacked the words to properly explain how much his unshakable presence meant to her. Wishing she could say more, she brushed her fingers over his and whispered, "Thank you for going with me today."

He smiled and brushed a kiss on her cheek. "Thanks for letting me be there."

When he left, she couldn't wipe the smile off her face. Her mother was smiling too. "That's a good man, Katherine. I have a feeling when he goes to college we won't be seeing the last of him."

And as greedy as it was to hope that Anthony might hold a bit of his life back to suit hers, she hoped her mother was right.

CHAPTER 13

Ant returned to the hardware store on cloud nine. Seeing the baby was incredible. His response might have been irrational, being that Kate's baby wasn't his, but he'd never felt so proud. A son. Kate was having a son.

The bell at the front of the store jingled as he tied his apron around his waist and went to help the customers. An older man was looking for paint to match a dresser that had some chips in it and he cheerfully mixed up a quart for him.

Just as he was finishing up the order, the bell jingled again and he kept an ear out to see what the next customer might need while bagging the paint.

"I'll be with you in a minute," he called, not yet seeing the customer.

The man rounded the corner and said, "Do you guys carry weed whacker string?"

The second he saw who it was every pleasant feeling inside of him died. Face slack, lips numb, he mumbled, "Yeah. Aisle nine."

The guy nodded and disappeared in that direction. Ant waited at the register, unable to move to help the customer like he usually did. When the customer returned, string in hand, Ant had to force himself to take the order and scan it into the register.

His hands trembled as the other man's scent filled the air. Within a split second he'd sized up everything he disliked about him down to the way he laced his shoes. Memories of Kate's stories came back to him. Though it had been a while since he saw her look anything but happy, he'd never forget how sad she looked the day she told him about her "friend's" first time.

"Don't I know you?"

Ant couldn't force the customary smile he gave the other patrons. "We graduated together."

"That's right. Ant Marcelli." The sound of his voice grated over every nerve. "I didn't know you worked here."

Ant didn't comment. "That's six seventy-five."

The guy put a ten-dollar bill on the counter. "You're friends with Kate McCullough, right?"

His shoulders tensed and he nearly lost the feather light hold he had on his temper. That he even assumed the right to speak her name pissed him off. For months the guy had acted like she didn't exist, left her to handle so much on her own when she was damn well entitled to demand he compensate for his part. But Katie wasn't that sort of girl. She had too much pride and more than enough independence to figure things out on her own without this piece of shit making her feel bad.

"She's my girlfriend."

All jovialness left the other man's face and he blinked dumbly. "She's dating?"

Ant met his gaze, every ounce of his being seething to let loose. "I know who you are, Nick."

Nick's jaw twitched, but he kept silent. Ant handed him his change.

"I, uh…" The guy took his bag and hesitated. "Tell Kate I said I hope she's doing okay."

"She's doing fine," Ant informed him, narrowing his eyes. "We have everything under control." Even that little bit of assurance felt like more than the guy deserved, but Ant would be damned if he let him walk away somehow assuming she might be less without him. "She's never been happier." *And you get no credit for that happiness, asshole.*

Nick frowned and nodded, slowly backing out of the store.

By the time Ant's shift was over his face hurt from grimacing. How could that guy act like he had nothing to do with a baby he created? Forget the fact that he was missing out, because that left room for Ant in Kate's life. But didn't he want to know about his child?

Ant debated telling Kate that he'd run into Nick, but thought better of it. He didn't want to stress her out. It made no difference anyway. It was clear Nick was *not* going to be involved or even admit the slightest responsibility for his part in their situation.

That night they ate at his house and followed dinner with a game of Five Hundred Rummy. His parents were big gamblers and loved to play cards over coffee. Kate was so great, laughing and teasing his father. Though his dad never commented on her situation, Ant believed Kate was so lovable his dad found her pregnancy hard to hold it against them.

After she left, he rummaged through the cabinets for a snack and his father called him from the back lawn. "Ant?"

He stepped out back and found his dad sitting on the patio furniture drinking a beer. He held an unopened bottle out to him. Ant took the beer and sat beside him, sipping in companionable silence.

"She's a sweet girl."

"Yup." More than sweet. She was everything a girl should be.

"You love her?"

Ant nodded, unsure if he'd ever be able to hide how much. "Definitely."

There was another long beat of silence. "Is it really yours, Anthony?"

He looked at his father, not saying a word, but telling him with his eyes that whatever conclusion he drew made no difference in his feelings for Kate. Wanting to be perfectly clear, he muttered, "Does it matter, Dad?"

"I'd think it should."

"Why? I'm not going to leave her because she has a

child. She's not going to leave me because I'm going to college. What difference does a paternity test make?"

His dad grunted. "Kids are expensive, Anthony. I break my back putting your sisters through private school. And your tuition's no joke."

"The baby's not even born yet, Pop. There's plenty of time to worry about saving up for college."

"You're young. You've got a lot of opportunity ahead of you. I don't want to see you throwing it away."

He finished his beer. "I'm not. I'm seizing every chance I get to go after what I want." He stood. "I know you're looking out, but this is my life. You got to live yours the way you wanted and now it's my turn to live mine."

"Anthony," his dad called as he started back toward the house. "I like her. But I *love* my children. I've always done everything in my power to make your lives easier. That took some sacrifice on my part. Sometimes we have to let things in our past go to have a better future."

He looked at his father a moment longer, struggling to put his feelings into words. He understood his point. Knew that Kate's situation complicated his plans, but he also knew he couldn't let her go and no matter what he might sacrifice to be with her, nothing would be worse than being without her. "She is my future, Pop."

ANT STARED at the housing paperwork feeling like there was an albatross around his neck. The deadline was tomorrow and as much as he had a choice in the matter, the decision was already made for him. With the little he earned at the hardware store and the cost of commuting, he'd be living off pennies trying to travel back and forth. Not to mention the time it would take to commute. He had to go.

His grip tightened on the pencil in his hand, snapping it in half. He shoved the paperwork away only to pull it back again. He was out of time.

Gritting his teeth, he signed the form and sealed it in the envelope. As he dropped it in the mail his stomach twisted with awareness. No turning back. Unable to face his imminent future, he avoided the house and got in his car, driving straight to Kate's.

After dinner they sat on the porch like they usually did. It was the only private place in a house of nine.

"You're quiet tonight," she whispered.

"I have some things on my mind."

She leaned her head on his shoulder as they rocked slowly on the swing. "Wanna talk about it?"

"I sent in my housing paperwork today." The longer he waited for some sense of rightness, the more certain he was it wouldn't come.

She didn't comment, but he knew she understood what this meant for them. After a while she said, "I could come visit you and you could come home on the weekends."

"I know."

There seemed nothing more to say beyond the endless

promises that they would try and the knowledge that things would dramatically change. They barely spoke that night, the weight of their worries almost too much to bear. When he drove home he accepted no comfort would ever come from his decision and true grief took hold.

His confidence was truly tested in the days that followed. His mother started a pile in the dining room of things he'd need to take to his dorm. Everything was moving too fast and no matter how he tried he couldn't make time slow down. His mother constantly asked his opinion on furnishings, but he didn't care about any of that, didn't want to think about a home Kate wasn't a part of.

When Kate saw all the bedding and buildable shelves piled up in the dining room, worry flashed in her eyes. She tried to act excited and interested, but it was all an act for his sake, one he didn't need. As she perused one item after another he thought about the day all the baby items arrived in her room. This should have been just as exciting, but it sucked.

"Come on," he said, not wanting to look at the piles anymore. "Let's take a walk." Normally they talked when they went on walks, but that day Kate stayed quiet.

August arrived and the shift in their relationship was impossible to ignore. Kate continued to see him, but her mood was subdued. He wished there was a way to go to school and still see her every day, but unless he switched to a closer college or dropped half his course load, he was out of ideas.

One night, mid-August and exactly one week before he left for school, she broke down and cried in his arms. He tried to comfort her, but nothing he said seemed to help.

"Things won't change between us, Katie. I know we won't see each other as much, but I'll love you just the same, and when we do see each other it will be that much better."

"I know." She sniffled and wiped her eyes. She hung her head and whispered, "I don't want to talk about it."

"Hey." He lifted her chin so she would look at him. "Don't shut me out. Tell me why you're upset."

It took a lot of coaxing, but eventually she opened up. "There are going to be other women there. Smart, single, beautiful women."

"You don't have to worry about that."

"Anthony, we have to be realistic. I love you, but…" She struggled through her tears. "You're my best friend. I know we love each other, but we've only been together that one time, and maybe that's the way it should be."

"Kate, I *love* you. We're more than friends. Sex doesn't validate anything." He pointed to his chest. "It's what we feel in here."

True they had only shared that one incredible night, but that had more to do with their living situations than anything else. She was pregnant and he couldn't very well make love to her in the back of his car—though there were plenty of times he wanted to.

She nodded, lowering her head again. "I just want you to know that if you met someone else…I'd understand."

"Hey, look at me." He cupped her face and pressed his lips to hers, softly whispering, "There won't be anyone else. You're it."

She leaned into him and shyly pulled him closer. He kissed her deeply, trying to convey everything he felt for her and how sexy he found her. His hand grazed her swollen belly as he gently cupped her breast and massaged softly.

She breathlessly sighed against his lips, her hands needy as they moved over his clothes. Once again he had to pull back. They were on her porch. Anyone could walk out at any moment. They sat back and stared at the field as the sun set, their frustration palpable.

"Let's go away this week," he suddenly said.

"You're leaving on Saturday."

"Before then. Let's go somewhere."

"Anthony, we don't have the money for that."

"I have money. I can take a little out of my savings and we'll rent a room. I want to be with you again before I go."

She looked down at her stomach. "Maybe we should just leave things as they are."

He frowned, not liking the hopelessness he caught in her tone. "Why?"

"Because of everything I just said. That night in June was perfect."

"There will be more nights like that, Kate. It can be like

that again. Trust me. It will be. That night had nothing to do with timing and everything to do with us."

She sighed, a small dimple forming in her cheek as her mouth twisted. "I'm fat."

"Shut up. You are *not* fat. You're really being down on yourself."

When she looked away, a horrible knot tightened in his gut. "Kate. What's going on? Tell me the truth."

"We said it would just be the summer. Every day it hurts more and more to think of you gone. I just want the hurting to stop."

The sickening knot twisted tighter and immense pressure filled his chest. "Are you breaking up with me?"

The apology in her eyes was clear. "I love you, Anthony. I love you so much that I can't bear to hold you back."

"You're not," he snapped. "Jesus, Kate. Knock it off. Everything's fine the way it is."

"You say that now, because we're here and everything's calm and quiet, but when you're there everything will be busy and fast. Your days will fly by like minutes while mine progress like years. At first you'll call, but then something will come up—"

"I'll call. I'll fucking call. What are you doing? This is pointless."

"This is being realistic," she argued.

He shot to his feet, too panicked to sit. "Then I won't go. I'll stay here and commute. I don't care about living there. I care about you."

"You have to go. This is what you planned, what you promised your parents."

"I don't care. I'm not going unless I know we'll be fine."

Her lips pressed tight as she glanced away.

He crouched in front of her and gripped her hands, desperation making him tremble. "Kate, listen to me. We are *not* breaking up. If I could, I'd take you with—" His words cut off, his thoughts derailing and moving in a total opposite direction. "You could come with me."

"I live *here*, Anthony. I can't afford to move out and raise a baby. I don't have enough money and I work here."

He shook his head. It was so simple, but a huge leap of faith. "They have family housing."

"For students!"

"No, for the students that have families. I have a scholarship. They'd pay for whatever dorm my needs qualified for. You could live with me."

She frowned at him. "They won't allow that."

"They would if you were my wife."

Her hands yanked out of his and she stood so fast he nearly fell back. "Stop it, Anthony. We aren't getting married."

"Why? I love you. I want to be with you. You're having a baby."

"Yes, I'm having a *baby*! Do you hear that? Me. I'm having another man's baby and you're out of your mind."

He knew it was a stretch, but he wasn't expecting her rejection to cut so deep. "You wouldn't marry me?"

Her shoulders sagged. "Anthony, we're too young to get married."

"Who says? Your mom married your dad at your age. My parents got married when they were twenty-one. We're adults." He hoped this would bring her comfort, but she looked sadder now than she had five minutes ago.

"No. The answer's no."

He should have gone to her, but her blunt rejection cut him down, and he couldn't find the strength to comfort her when his heart was bleeding on the inside. Swallowing, he stepped back and reached in his pocket for his keys.

"You act like marrying me would make you miserable, Kate. I know we're young and we wouldn't have a lot of money, but I'd be a good husband. I'd treat your son like he was my own and I'd love you and him with every part of my being. I'd always put you before me, but sometimes…" He shook his head and laughed without humor. "Sometimes you make that impossible. I have to go."

Since the beginning he'd been chasing her, begging her to take a chance on him. He'd hoped they were past all the second guessing, hoped the idea of making a memorable summer and calling it quits was just some asinine plan they had in the beginning. That maybe their connection would prove love couldn't just be shut off. But here he was asking to *marry her* and she didn't even have the conviction to stay together as a couple.

When he reached his house he felt utterly foolish and severely ripped off. She'd rather end everything they had than take a chance on working to make it last. Marriage wasn't even enough security for her to be happy.

He never let his ego get in the way of reality, but she could be such a pain in the ass when she got stubborn. He didn't understand how, when she obviously loved him and wanted to be with him, she'd view breaking up as any sort of solution. It wasn't.

When he entered his room a box sat on his bed. Peeking inside he saw more shit for school. Frustrated, he flung out his hand and threw the box on the floor. *"Fuck!"* He fell back on his bed and gritted his teeth, resenting every bit of opportunity ahead of him.

Kate tossed and turned in bed long after midnight. When sleep proved utterly impossible, she went to the kitchen to find something to eat. Strangely, even food didn't bring her peace. As she stared out the back window, her conversation with Anthony played like a broken record in her head and her heart broke a little more each time she thought about what she'd said to him.

She didn't want to break up with him, but it seemed the right thing to do. She was holding him back and eventually he'd leave her behind, because their lives—like they'd always been—were moving in opposite directions.

Knowing she'd done the right thing and made one of the hardest choices in her life should have made her feel better. It was supposed to end the pain, cut off the agonizing anticipation of their inevitable end, but the ache she felt now was worse than anything that came before.

Her head tipped back as she looked up at the ceiling. Her parents were asleep and no one was there to tell her she'd done the right thing. Worst of all, she'd hurt Ant, a guy who had been incredible to her since day one. If she could just explain that this was for the best, make him understand and accept reality, she'd feel better.

Her hand slid over the counter and gripped her car keys. It was late and dark, but something inside of her knew she wouldn't rest until she made this right. She had to make him see this was the only way it could be, no matter how much it crushed them.

She quietly left the house. The streets were empty and the world had an eerie sense of nothingness as she drove to his house. So not to wake his parents, she parked across the street and waited for her common sense to kick in. It didn't.

Looking at the clock on the dashboard, she winced. The house was dark and it was too late to knock. She studied the windows and was pretty sure the one on the bottom left side was his room, but if she was wrong this could end disastrously.

Climbing out of the car, she crept through his yard and drew in several deep breaths. She looked for a pebble to throw, but there was nothing but grass. Stepping over the shrubs, she stared up at the window, which was higher than it seemed from the road. She tapped lightly.

This was stupid. She was going to make a fool of

herself or worse, wake up the entire house. Turning away, she stepped over a shrub and stilled as a light flipped on inside the house. Crap. Her heartbeat turned frantic as she stood like a bandit in the dark as the window slid open.

"Kate?" *Annnnd that was not Anthony.*

She slowly turned. "Hey Angela. Sorry to wake you."

Anthony's little sister grinned. "Are you looking for my brother?"

"Um…yeah. But I can just call him in the morning."

His sister shrugged and pointed to her right. "His window's that one."

Kate nodded, wishing she could shrink away and pretend this never happened. "I'm gonna go. Please don't tell anyone I was here."

The girl smiled. "I won't, but I think it's totally romantic. My parents sleep like the dead. You want me to get him for you?"

"No. I'll just talk to him tomorrow." She had to get out of there.

"Okay. I'll see you later."

"Goodnight."

Creeping over the lawn, she made her way back to the front of the house, mentally cursing herself the entire time. She was such an idiot.

"Did you just come to talk to my little sister?"

Spinning on her heels she gasped and stared as Antony sat on the front stoop. "I didn't mean to come here."

"Sleepwalking again?"

She laughed and hung her head. "I couldn't sleep."

"Me neither." He stood. "Come in. We'll talk."

Hesitating, she took a slow step forward. "I could just call you tomorrow."

"Kate, stop being difficult. Come inside."

She followed him through the dark house and into his room. When he shut the door her thoughts scattered and she couldn't remember what was so pressing that couldn't wait until morning. He sat beside her on the bed.

"You wanna go first?"

She nodded then shook her head. "I'm so confused, Anthony."

"Me too."

Being that he always seemed so calm and in command, she found that hard to believe. "You are?"

"Yeah. Kate, I don't have all the answers. I'm just trying to find the best solution."

"I can't marry you, Anthony."

His gaze drifted away. "I know. That might have been a little extreme. But if you said yes, I'd still do it."

"I don't want to get married because it's convenient."

He sent her a sidelong glance. "It would have been for love, Katie, not convenience. I wouldn't have offered for any other reason."

"Your parents would never support that. It's too soon."

"Maybe," he agreed. "The funny thing is, once I put it on the table and you took it off I realized how much part of me truly wants to marry you. I know we're young, but... when I'm with you, I'm happier than when I'm anywhere else. I don't think about if there's a greater happiness or better places to be. I'm just… happy where I am—with you."

Her heart thundered as he put his feelings, as well as hers, into words perfectly. "I feel the same way."

His fingers closed over hand. "Then stop trying to break up with me."

She drew in a deep breath and let it out slowly. "I'm so afraid you'll miss something next year and resent me for it in the future."

"Babe, the only thing I'm going to miss is you."

"I don't want you to go." It was the first time she admitted it out loud and it crushed her to hear how selfish those words sounded. "I know you have to, but…I can't imagine not seeing you every day. It's going to kill me."

"Me too. But I'm not far and I promise I'll be back whenever I can. And just think, you can come see me, too. We might actually have more time alone than we do now."

"What about your roommate?"

"I'll kick him out," he laughed and she smiled as his dark gaze settled on hers. "Come here."

She turned her face to his and he gently kissed her, easing her back onto the bed. Her fingers slid through his hair as he lay beside her. As their mouths teased, his hands crept over her curves, caressing and petting. Soon she was pulling off his shirt and sliding her hands between their bodies. The moment her fingers curled around his flesh he sighed into her shoulder. "God, Kate…"

She stroked him slowly as his fingers slid into her panties, teasing gently and probing softly. She moaned as he pressed deeper, her legs falling open. He stripped away her clothes and kissed down her chest, resting his palms over the swell of her belly. Gazing down at him she smiled, wondering how anyone could be so wonderful. Although he wasn't the father, he'd stepped in and acted like he was in so many ways. It made it extremely difficult not to believe the fantasy.

Her hand reached for his, grasping his fingers and squeezing tenderly. "I love you, Anthony."

"I love you too, Katie."

Her eyes closed as his kisses traveled lower. Writhing, she savored every caress. Her fingers gripped the bedding as he brought her immeasurable pleasure. Finding a comfortable position was a bit of a challenge, but they figured it out. Rolling to her side, he fit his body behind hers and slowly filled her.

Their fingers laced together, holding tight as he gently took her. Her sighs were soft and with every advance his lips pressed kisses into her skin as he whispered words of love and adoration.

"I never want to give this up, Kate," he rasped, rolling her nipple slowly between his fingers. "Tell me we're safe. I need to know we're solid or I'll never be able to go."

"We're safe," she whispered, cupping her hand over his and holding him to her pounding heart. "We're safe."

He turned her face and caught her mouth in a kiss as he thrust one last time and trembled, his arms pulling her tight. "Stay with me tonight."

Her heart, with all its chips and fractures couldn't bear

the thought of leaving. Nodding, she turned and looked into his eyes. "I'll stay."

KATE STAYED at his house every night that week. Neither of their parents seemed to mind, or if they did, none of them dared to comment. Friday night was the hardest, as it was the last night before he left for school. They made love several times and Kate cried long after Anthony fell asleep. No matter how much she tried to avoid this moment, it was happening. He was leaving.

The ride to the campus was too short, but in a way, that was reassuring. Though she couldn't carry much, she did help with unpacking and situating his desk. Ant's roommate, a kid named Jack, was big into sports and already settled, being that the athletes arrived earlier for training. He seemed nice and Kate was glad he didn't impose on them while they got Anthony settled.

His mother was a wreck, lingering for a solid hour after his father stated it was time to leave. His sisters hadn't come with them and Anthony tolerated an embarrassing amount of kisses before his father finally peeled his mom away and shuffled her off to the car.

When he finally shut the door and they were alone, he sighed. "I thought they'd never leave."

Kate smiled, but it cost her. She was next to go. "Are you nervous?"

"More anxious."

"What will you do tomorrow?"

He shrugged. "Walk around, figure out where my classes are, and buy my books." He sat beside her on the small dorm bed. "You could stay if you want."

She'd thought about it, but with his roommate there and all the times she used the bathroom in the middle of the night, she didn't want to start him off on the wrong foot with the rest of the dorm. "No, that wouldn't be fair to Jack. Maybe next weekend."

"Do you want to come with me to the cafeteria for dinner before you go?"

They dined on college fare and part of her was envious of the experience he was getting. On their walk back to the dorms, she held his hand. "This is really exciting, Anthony. You're going to love it here."

"Let's just hope I can keep my GPA up."

"You will." If anything, Anthony was smart and devoted to his dreams.

When they reached the entrance to the dorms she hesitated.

"Aren't you coming back up?" he asked, worry playing in his eyes.

"It's getting late. I don't want to drive home in the dark."

The ease he held all day seemed to fade. "I hate this part."

She hated it too. "We'll see each other in six days." It would be the longest six days of her life. How would they ever survive four years of this?

He walked her to her car and kissed her for several minutes at the door. "I'll miss you."

"I'll miss you too."

His hand rested on her stomach. "And I'll miss him." He smirked and spoke to her belly. "You be good for your mother."

She laughed so she wouldn't cry. They always knew this would be the worst part. "I love you," she whispered, hugging him one last time.

"Call me when you get home. You wrote down my new number, right?"

"Yes, I have it."

He opened the car door and waited as she rolled down her window and buckled up. "Drive safe."

Six days. She'd see him in six days.

As she drove away he stood and watched her go, not moving until she turned out of the parking lot and lost sight of him. The drive home was made in loud sobs and the ugliest of cries as she listened to the Dave Matthews CD he gave her as loud as her stereo could go.

As promised, Anthony came back the following Friday. He had lots to say about college life and seemed to be having a ball. She was thrilled to have him home again, but Sunday came too soon. Another five days of waiting to go.

As the semester carried on, and they fell into a rhythm

of waiting out the hellos and suffering through the painful goodbyes, her second trimester came to a close. Her stomach seemed to grow by the minute and getting around became a challenge.

When midterms came, Anthony said he needed to study and asked if she could come there. She did, of course, but it was a terrible weekend. His bed was small and stiff and she hardly slept, which made her emotional and cranky. When she came home she was exhausted and worried.

Anthony was busier and busier as the weeks went on. It seemed he was always studying for something and the time he spent in class covered only a quarter of the work he had to accomplish on his own.

She started counting down the days to Thanksgiving break, looking forward to more than a short weekend with him. After that would come Christmas, and then he'd have one semester under his belt and only seven more to go. And she'd be a mother. It was daunting, to say the least.

Not only was she counting time on a school schedule, she was losing time to prepare for her own challenges ahead. Every night she worried about crazy things like childbirth and who would be there when the baby was born. What if she had the baby during finals and Anthony couldn't make it back? That was one of her greatest fears, because she wanted him there as much as she needed her own family present—maybe more.

As the seasons changed and the leaves turned, she

accepted that she wasn't going to wear anything stylish for some time. Her wardrobe had shifted to shades of pastel and horrid floral prints and she worried Ant would come home and be completely turned off.

The morning before Thanksgiving she spent extra time getting ready, curling her hair and putting on more makeup than she typically wore. She borrowed her mother's earrings, the ones he liked, and tried not to spill anything on her shirt. But nothing disguised the fact that she looked like a wobbly bowling pin.

"Are you excited for Anthony to come home, love?" Her Aunt Colleen asked as she and her mother peeled potatoes for the big feast.

"I feel like a cow."

Her aunt tsked. "Nonsense, you're glowing."

With every worry came the constant sense that she was having a child in a few weeks. She was a ticking time bomb.

Anthony made it to Center County around noon, but had to do some things at home before he could come over. "Do you want me to come there? I could help," she offered over the phone. She was so eager to see him, she didn't mind doing some extra work.

"No. I shouldn't be long. I promise I'll be there in a couple hours."

A couple of hours? Disappointed, she returned to helping her aunts and her mother prepare for Thanksgiving. When Anthony finally arrived, he was beaming. He hugged her and touched her stomach and immediately all her worries about her changing body disappeared.

They sat on the couch, her shirt pulled up to her ribs and watched the baby kick. "Holy crap!" Anthony cheered when her stomach rippled as the baby moved. "He's going to be a linebacker."

She laughed. "Maybe his Uncle Luke can teach him how to play."

His head cocked to the side as he sent her a strange look. "Maybe I can."

"That too."

Her father came into the living room searching for his shoes. "Paulie's car broke down again. I have to go get him."

"Do you need a hand?" Anthony asked and Kate frowned. He just got there.

"Sure. Grab your coat."

Ant looked back at her. "Do you care if I go?"

She couldn't mask her disappointment. "I guess not. Try not to be long though."

He kissed her and followed her dad out of the house. She wasn't sure why it seemed impossible to keep him in one place, but she was getting really irritated with waiting for him to return.

As the door closed, her sister came into the living room and plopped in Anthony's empty spot. "Your stomach's *huge*."

Kate's mouth pursed. "Thanks."

Sheilagh eyed her belly as the baby kicked. "I think

you're having an alien."

She rolled her eyes. "I think you're about as tactful as a goat."

Her baby sister shrugged, her pigtails lopsided from playing all day. "He's growing lungs, you know."

Kate's brow lifted. She did know, but was surprised her little sister had such information. "That's true."

"And he's getting fat so he'll be warm when he's not in your belly anymore."

"How do you know that?"

She bit her thumbnail and Kate scrunched her nose, as her little fingers didn't look freshly washed. "I read it in that book." She pointed to the large pregnancy manual on the table.

Kate wasn't surprised. Sheilagh had been reading since she was four and helped herself to anything lying around the house. "That book's a little old for you."

"Our insides look like a cow." She reached forward and paged through the book, showing Kate the illustration of the female anatomy. It did look like the face of a cow, the fallopian tubes making up the ears.

"Boys don't have cows in their bellies. They have other things."

Kate laughed, lowering her shirt. "You're so weird."

Again, Sheilagh shrugged, as if this wasn't news. "Your baby's gonna have a dingle. That's what boys have."

"You know too much."

She turned, her green eyes bright as a wicked smirk

stretched her pudgy cheeks. "When I punch Kelly in the dingle he cries like a little girl."

"Don't do that."

"Why?"

Kate laughed. "Because it's not good."

Sheilagh shrugged again. "He stole my bike and wouldn't give it back."

Taking a deep breath as if it somehow added to the reserve of patience she'd need for the trials ahead, she said, "Well, don't go punching your nephew in the dingle."

Her little lips parted. "He's gonna be my nephew?"

"Yeah."

"Will he call me Aunt Sheilagh?"

"If you want him too."

Her eyes shifted as she smiled again. "Like a grown-up." Sliding off the couch, she ran out of the room. "Mum! I'm gonna be an aunt!"

Kate eased back on the couch and shut her eyes, laughing to herself. Her hand rested affectionately on her belly. "I won't let your aunt beat you up."

An hour later, Anthony and her father were back, but the whole family was home and she felt claustrophobic. "Do you want to watch a movie in my room or something?" She just wanted some time alone with him.

"Sure—"

"Ant," her dad called, standing in the doorway. "Can you give me a hand with something in the barn?"

"We were just going to watch a movie, Dad. Can Colin help you?"

"It'll only take a second."

Anthony stood and, once again, she was being kissed goodbye. "I'll be right back."

She scoffed and as they disappeared she mumbled, "I guess I'll be right here—waiting."

ANTHONY FOLLOWED Kate's dad out to the barn, his heart racing like it had since that morning.

"Shut the door," Frank said, the moment they were inside.

He closed the heavy doors and faced the man he'd once found terrifying. He was still scary, but now Anthony understood the whole of him and knew he was more gentle hearted than anything else, especially when it came to his family.

"You sure about this?" Frank asked. "I won't hold it against you if you're rethinking things. I know your intentions were honorable."

Ant smiled, never being surer about anything else in his life. "I wouldn't have asked if I wasn't sure."

Frank nodded and slid a small box across the workbench. "It's not much. My mother wasn't a fancy woman and I lost a lot of her things after my father passed."

Ant's hands were unsteady as he reached for the box, prying it open with a creak. It wasn't anything elegant, just a simple sapphire on a silver band, but it was more valuable than anything he could afford on his own. "I think it's perfect. Thank you, Frank—for everything."

When he'd asked Frank for his blessing that morning, he worried the man would say no, telling him it was too soon and things were too complicated. Never in a million years did he expect to see Frank's composure slip and the man nod tightly on the verge of tears.

"You're good to her, Ant. That ever changes, we'll have a problem. But you keep taking care of her the way you do, being there for her when it counts, and my blessing will hold. We'll help you two out anyway we can." He laughed, and patted his shoulder with his big mitt of a hand. "You'll need all the help you can get. She's more like her mother than most realize."

He grinned and pocketed the ring. "I hope I never let you *or her* down."

"Me too."

When he returned to the house Kate was in a mood. He felt guilty for pushing her off the first day he was home, but he wanted to take care of this. He'd made up his mind back in October when school had interfered with their time. There was no reason for them to waste another minute. They loved each other and she was going to be his wife sooner or later. His entire week was focused on convincing her to marry him and he wasn't going back until that ring was on her finger.

"How about that movie?"

"Are you sure you don't want to help anyone else? My brothers are cleaning their rooms and could use a hand—"

He kissed her until she softened, her anger slowly fading. "Stop. I'm not going anywhere. You have me until tomorrow morning."

"I better." She pouted, but forgiveness showed in her eyes.

They watched *An Affair to Remember* and Kate predictably fell asleep halfway through. He'd told his parents he was sleeping at the McCullough's, but he hardly slept a wink that night, his brain constantly thinking of the best way to propose and, hopefully, this time, get a yes. He should wait a few days and set up something nice, but knowing her, she'd be more upset if he excluded her from his plans again.

By morning, he was still tossing and turning when he heard her get out of bed. Knowing she'd only be gone a few minutes, he grabbed his jeans off the floor and removed the ring from the box. A few minutes later she returned and slipped back under the covers.

He pulled her close. "I love waking up with you."

She hummed and rolled to face him. "Me too. Happy Thanksgiving."

"I'm most thankful for you."

The house was drafty and the sky was gray. Chances were they'd get their first snow by nightfall. Pulling the covers to their shoulders, he found her hands resting on her belly. He placed his fingers over hers and chuckled as he felt the slightest flutter of a kick. Counting out her fingers, he lifted the one next to her pinky and slipped the ring over her knuckle. "Let's wake up every morning together, Kate. Forever."

She frowned and pulled her hand out from the covers. "Where did you get this?"

"Do you recognize it?"

"It was my grandmother's." Her gaze shot to his. "Anthony…what is this?"

"Yesterday I didn't want to just help your dad fix your uncle's car. I wanted to ask him an important question." His heart pounded as he sent a prayer to God that she wouldn't overreact and think him high-handed. "I love you, Kate. I want to marry you." His hand returned to her stomach. "I want this baby to be ours and I want us to be a family. Will you marry me?"

"But school—"

"Will be there. It's not an excuse, Kate. This semester's been trying enough. How many more do we have to go through apart when nothing's stopping us from being together?"

She looked back at the ring. "What did my dad say?"

"He was more than happy to give us his blessing, but he warned me that you have a lot of your mother in you."

She laughed. "He's right."

"Say yes. Enough wasting time. We can get married this winter and we can move into the family housing by next semester, you, our son, and me—together, the way a family should be. Please do this for us."

Her face pinched as a single tear rolled to her nose, her head slightly nodding.

"Is that a yes?"

She sniffled and giggled. "Yes. I'll marry you, Anthony."

His grin broke wide as he tipped his head back and laughed. "Finally!" he roared, pulling her to him and kissing her hard. "You're a stubborn woman, but you're *my* stubborn woman. I knew I'd get through to you eventually."

She giggled and looked into his eyes. "Are you sure this is what you want?"

"Sure? Woman, I've been trying to sell you on being my girl since the day we met. Yes, I'm sure!"

She bit her lip, her cheeks tight with a grin. "We're getting married."

He nodded, so many worries laid to rest. "Yes, we are."

"After finals?"

He thought for a minute. "It depends what kind of wedding you want."

"I don't care about the wedding. I just want you."

"Then we don't have to wait. We could get a license and go down to the court house this week if you wanted."

"I'll have to talk to my mom about that. Her heart might be set on seeing me married in a church."

He didn't want to wait too long. Lowering his voice, he looked her in the eyes. "Kate, I want to talk to Nick about signing over custody of the baby. I don't ever want this child to feel different than any of our other children. He'll be *our* son. Nick's just a shadow hanging over our heads and I won't feel secure that I can protect my family until I'm certain he can't interfere."

Her gaze lowered. "That would require him putting his name on something that legally traces him back to the baby."

"But it would also legally remove his rights. I know you don't want to involve him, but it's what needs to be done. If you don't want to face him, I will."

"I don't think he'll put up much of a fight."

The sad part was she was right. Nick would be a simple obstacle, but down the line he might change and Ant couldn't risk him coming back and jeopardizing their family or Kate's happiness.

"Let me handle it. All you'll have to do is sign an agreement in front of a notary."

"How do you know that's all it involves?"

"Because I already looked into it. I told you I was serious. I know what I want and I don't intend to let anything or anyone stand in my way."

She pressed her forehead to his. "What did I ever do to deserve you?"

"I ask myself the same thing every day."

THE CEREMONY WAS HELD on a Tuesday at their family's church. The ground was covered in snow as their families trickled in and became one. Kate didn't know what made him love her the way he did. She wasn't sure how his parents had raised such an honorable man. But she knew without a doubt, that Anthony would be an incredible husband and father and teach their son how to be just as honorable.

"Do you take this woman to be your lawfully wedded wife, to have and to hold, from this day forward, for better, for worse, for richer, for poorer, in sickness and in health?"

"I do."

The priest looked at her and asked the same. She never believed in a promise as much as she believed in the one she made that day. She'd love him through the fiercest storms and hold onto him during the darkest hours. No matter what lay ahead, they'd face it together, always and forever. Because deep in her heart, beside all the folly and confusion, she knew one truth to be absolute, she loved him with every ounce of her being and Anthony knew how to love her exactly the way she needed to be loved.

"I do."

"Push, Katie! Push!"

Kate gripped the rails of the bed and gritted her teeth. So help her God, this child was getting out of her tonight! It was Christmas Eve, sixteen days past her actual due date.

"Come on, dearie!"

"Someone dab her with the cloth before that vein in her forehead bursts," her aunt called and her mother and mother-in-law shoved the doctor aside to get to her before anyone else.

"That's it!" the doctor snapped. "I need everyone who's not the father to get out."

Her mother, her mother-in-law, the aunts, Anthony's nonna, and her grandmother balked. "We're just tryin' to help."

The doctor looked back at them, but Kate was practically having an asthma attack through her contraction and couldn't exactly waste her breath on words.

"Anthony, tell him we can stay," his mother demanded.

He shook his head, so patient and firm. "Sorry, Ma. I promise we'll bring him out as soon as he gets here, but there are just too many of you."

This might have been the first time Anthony had ever dared to tell his mother no. She didn't take it well. "How could you take this away from me? My first grandson!"

"No one's taking anything away from you. Katie needs some space and I intend to make sure she has it. We'll call you back as soon as we can."

The six affronted women shuffled out of the delivery room mumbling and shaking their heads. "Thank you," Kate rasped, in between contractions.

"Are we ready now?" the doctor asked. "I think we have one or two more pushes before you meet your son."

She nodded, bearing down as another contraction took hold. It was *not* pleasant, but there was nothing quite as incredible as hearing those first little squawks as her son drew in his first breath.

Anthony smiled, his eyes glassy as the nurse placed their son in her arms. She couldn't believe he was finally here. Her beautiful baby boy. Anthony leaned over and kissed his head then kissed hers, his voice a mere rasp. "You did it, baby."

Kate looked up at him. A thousand beautiful emotions running through her at once. "*We* did it."

"Do you have a name?" the nurse asked.

Kate smiled up at her husband, happier than she'd ever dreamed she'd be. Anthony nodded and told the nurse, "We're going to call him Frank, after his grandfather."

Weak from such a long labor Kate sighed, overflowing with absolute contentment. "He's perfect."

"Yes, he is." Ant leaned close and spoke softly. "Hey, little guy. I'm your daddy. We're gonna play football together and your mom's gonna teach you to hunt."

As he went on, promising the world to their little boy, Kate stared at him, incapable of counting all the blessings she had. Though their engagement had been an untraditional one and their start a bit different from what most expected, she knew without a doubt that this was where she belonged. Their first home would be small, but eventually they'd return to the mountain and all of these little bumps along the way would be smoothed over by time.

Anthony somehow made her believe that normal wasn't always better. And like her mother said, love was messy. She loved her life more then than she ever thought possible, all the mess, all the emotion, and all the unusual parts coming together to make what she considered a pretty perfect whole.

Anthony took Frank in his arms and nestled his little face with his nose. "You look like a McCullough, but don't you worry. We're gonna bring out the Marcelli in you yet."

THE END

If you enjoyed the McCullough Mountain series, you will

love the Jasper Falls series! Jasper Falls is the town at the foot of McCullough Mountain. Check out Jasper Falls and find out how the rest of the stories end!

<u>Wake My Heart</u> 1
<u>The Best Man</u> 2
<u>Love Me Nots</u> 3
<u>Pining For You</u> 4
<u>My Funny Valentine</u> 5
<u>Side Squeeze</u> 6
And many more…

ABOUT THE AUTHOR

Never miss another book release!
Click here to sign up for Lydia Michaels' Newsletter.

Follow Lydia Michaels on Instagram and Facebook!

What to Read Next?
Click here to claim your FREE Book from Lydia Michaels!

Billionaire Romance
Falling In | Sacrifice of the Pawn | Calamity Rayne

Small Town Romance
Wake My Heart | The Best Man | Love Me Nots | Pining
For You | Almost Priest

Emotional Favorites
La Vie en Rose | Simple Man | Wake My Heart | Sacrifice
of the Pawn | Forfeit

Romantic Comedy
Calamity Rayne

Erotic Romance
Breaking Perfect | Protégé | Falling In | Sugar

First Books in Binge Worthy Trilogies and Series
Almost Priest | Falling In | Wake My Heart | Forfeit | Original Sin

Paranormal Vampire Romance
Original Sin | Dark Exodus | Prodigal Son

LGBTQ+ & Menage Romance
Broken Man (MM) | Breaking Perfect (MMF) | Forfeit (MMF) | Hurt (Non-Consensual) | Protege

Sexy Nerds & Second Chances
Blind | Untied

Teacher Student, Workplace, and Age-Gap Love Affairs… Oh my!
British Professor | Pining For You | Breaking Perfect | Falling In | Sacrifice of the Pawn

Single Dads & Single Moms
Simple Man | Pining For You | First Comes Love | Controlled Chaos | Intentional Risk

Dark Psychological Thriller & Tortured Hero Romance
(TRIGGER WARNING)
Hurt

About the Author

Lydia Michaels is the award winning and bestselling author of more than forty titles. She is the consecutive winner of the 2018 & 2019 *Author of the Year Award* from *Happenings Media,* as well as the recipient of the 2014 *Best Author Award* from the *Courier Times.* She has been featured in *USA Today, Romantic Times Magazine, Love & Lace,* and more. As the host and founder of the *East Coast Author Convention,* the *Behind the Keys Author Retreat,* and *Read Between the Wines,* she continues to celebrate her growing love for readers and romance novels around the world.

In 2021, Michaels released the groundbreaking, non-fiction series, **Write 10K in a Day,** to commemorate her career in the publishing industry. She looks forward to many more years of exploring both fiction and non-fiction writing, teaching about the craft, and learning from the others in the author community.

Lydia is happily married to her childhood sweetheart. Some of her favorite things include the scent of paperback books, listening to her husband play piano, escaping to her coastal home at the Jersey Shore, cheap wine, *Game of*

Thrones, coffee, and kilts. She hopes to meet you soon at one of her many upcoming events.

You can follow Lydia at www.Facebook.com/LydiaMichaels or on Instagram @lydia_michaels_books

Other Titles by Lydia Michaels
Wake My Heart
The Best Man
Love Me Nots
Pining For You
My Funny Valentine
Falling In: Surrender Trilogy 1
Breaking Out: Surrender Trilogy 2
Coming Home: Surrender Trilogy 3
Sacrifice of the Pawn: Billionaire Romance
Queen of the Knight: Billionaire Romance
Original Sin
Dark Exodus
Calamity Rayne: Gets a Life
Calamity Rayne: Back Again
La Vie en Rose
Breaking Perfect
FREE! - Blind
Untied
Almost Priest
Beautiful Distraction
Irish Rogue

British Professor
Broken Man
Controlled Chaos
Hard Fix
Intentional Risk
Hurt
Sugar
Simple Man
Protégé
Forfeit
Lost Together
Atonement
First Comes Love
If I Fall
Something Borrowed
Write 10K in a Day